Herbert Kastle was bo
has been an English t
copywriter, but he nov
Kastle is the author of
The Movie Maker, *Cros*
and *Sunset People*.

By the same author

HERBERT KASTLE

Hot Prowl

PANTHER
Granada Publishing

Panther Books
Granada Publishing Ltd
8 Grafton Street, London W1X 3LA

Published by Panther Books 1977
Reprinted 1982, 1984, 1985

Copyright © Herbert Kastle 1965

ISBN 0-583-12763-0

Printed and bound in Great Britain by
Collins, Glasgow

Set in Intertype Times

FOR ESTELLE AND IRVING

CHAPTER ONE

He had known it was a mistake. Right from the beginning he had known that going away with Wallace for a week in the country wouldn't solve anything. But Laura had suggested it and Wallace had decided to be noble, and how could Ted fight his sister-in-law and brother-in-law when they were being noble and after they had done so much for him?

He was walking along the path leading to Pine Cliff. It had been a difficult climb yesterday, in midafternoon, and Wallace had given up after only a third of the way and collapsed on a boulder, shaking his head as sweat poured down his round, fleshy face. 'Too steep. Too hot. Let's forget it. Let's rest awhile and go back to the lodge.' But Ted had continued, and Wallace, suddenly afraid of leaving him alone, had staggered up a hundred feet more of winding path. There he had quit for good, his voice calling after Ted, pleading with him not to go too close to the edge of the cliff, not to 'do anything foolish'. Ted had climbed another half-hour before reaching the summit.

It had been tough then; it was tough now, in complete darkness. No moon, no stars – nothing penetrated the thick pine and the pin oak that pressed in on the narrow path.

He was strong enough, fresh enough. It was more comfortable, walking in the cool of night. And he was in excellent shape, having kept up his mat work and home exercises. But not being able to see more than a foot or two ahead brought him stumbling into trees and rocks and created a growing tension.

It was a few minutes to twelve by the luminous hands on his watch when the path leveled off and he came onto the flat-topped boulder, the thick lip of rock stuck out over a thousand feet of sheer cliffside. At the bottom was Lake Minnassa, a crater filled with icy water, a blackness that beckoned.

Yesterday he had stood looking down into the sunlit crater and the greenish-blue water. Yesterday he had stood in the little observation house, behind the roughhewn log railing, and felt the pull of that sheer drop, the promise of that icy water. Then three young men had arrived. One had brown hair and sharp, hard features and Ted had begun watching him from the corner of his eye. When the three youths had left, he had gone down after them; but he had known that the youth was too tall and too lean and after a while he had stopped and sat down on a fallen oak and smoked a cigarette.

Tonight he went past the observation house and moved to the edge of the rock itself. Tonight he was alone and there was no one to follow and the lake was black ... like the funeral guests' clothing that day when the two caskets, one pitifully small, were lowered into the raw earth and Laura wept and Wallace wept and all the black-clothed people wept and only he didn't weep.

He came closer, closer, taking tiny, shuffling steps until the tip of one shoe was over the edge. He bent forward, feeling a cool updraft. A little more, a little leaning outward, and there would be a swift falling, an icy end to the nightmares and the headaches, to the screams that only he could hear.

He thought of the boat boy, the short, tight-muscled teenager who had rented him a canoe after dinner. So close! Much closer than the boy yesterday. And with city accent and tough-guy swagger. He wanted to see that boy in normal clothing instead of the knee-length beachcomber Levi's that were his uniform of office.

A chill gust of air moved up from the chasm. He stepped back. He wondered if Wallace had awakened and found him gone. He hoped not. He didn't want to worry Wallace and have him call home and worry Laura.

He was going down the path now, and had to concentrate every ounce of mental power so he wouldn't lose his way. He stopped thinking of Wallace and Laura. He stopped thinking of anything. And this was good – the best time he'd had since coming to the lodge a week ago. He was glad it was ending with peace. Tomorrow they would drive back to New York and he would carry this final moment of peace with him.

The moment was aborted as a woman's laughter sounded somewhere off in the woods. In an instant his mind was filled with heated images. In an instant he burned for a woman. Susan. Edith Collers. The girls in tight stretch pants strolling the summer streets. The women in thin dresses filling the city with desire.

The path was leveling out. Soon he would pass the tennis court and reach the lodge: the old wood building with wide, circling porch, three stories high, and topped by towers and cupolas. The huge old building that slept early, that drowsed by ten and lay still and dead by eleven.

The guests were mostly elderly people. The younger ones came for a rest, as he had, or to accompany aging parents. There was no dancing, no drinking, no organized boy–girl business. But he had seen the waitresses and busboys, the kitchen help and other help, moving off in twos and fours. And now after a week of resting – of swimming and boating and hiking and eating and going to sleep early – now he had stopped thinking of that night and that boy and Laura and Wallace – stopped thinking and begun *sensing*.

There was movement in the woods about him, and movement in the building that loomed up ahead. Twenty-five waitresses and twelve busboys and other women in the kitchen and other men working around the lake and grounds. *They* didn't go to sleep by eleven or twelve. At breakfast they joked about being half dead. After dinner, they made their dates, pairing off.

There was a shortage of men. He had received enough smiles, enough quick glances, to know he wasn't canceled out by his age. Even Wallace, who hardly qualified as a make-out artist, received his share of promising looks from the plainer waitresses. But Wallace laughed it off. He felt that at thirty-five he was far too 'mature' for a twenty-year-old waitress. Kids, he called them. Cute kids or silly kids.

What would he think of Susan? Susan, who was only twenty-three.

The path forked into a broad dirt road, and up ahead yellow porch lights glimmered through an intervening stand of birch. He looked to his right, to where the tennis court lay in darkness. There was a bench at the far end. Players would sit there, talking, waiting their turns. Now there was silence, but he thought he saw movement.

He went on, as if unconcerned. He wondered if it was the

9

boathouse boy. He passed the courts and walked another thirty or forty feet, then left the road, cut right, passed through the stand of birch, and came out in high grass and woods. He cut right again and began walking behind the tennis court. He stopped, adjusting his vision, and saw the bench and what looked like a single figure. He dropped to his hands and knees and crawled up behind the bench.

The single figure divided in two – a boy and a girl. The girl said softly, 'No, please.' The boy put his face in her neck and murmured. The girl laughed but repeated, 'No.' The boy's head dropped. The girl sighed, leaning back against the wire fence. The boy's head dropped still farther.

Ted crawled a little past them to where he could look in from the side. He was no more than eight or ten feet away when he stopped. The boy was kissing the girl's knees. He pushed at her hand, which was pressing down her skirt. The hand came away and the girl sighed again, deeply, and the boy pushed her skirt up until the white of her thighs emerged. The boy kissed her thighs and the girl leaned farther back, face turned to the sky, lips twisted as if in pain. The boy raised his head, raised his body, leaned over the girl, pressing her back along the length of the bench. Ted saw him for an instant. It wasn't the boat boy. He had no reason to linger.

But now he wanted a girl. Now he was full of the redness of passion. Now he wanted to go to them and strike down the boy and tell the girl how much he wanted her, needed her . . .

The girl said, 'No,' sharply and squirmed aside and got up. The boy almost fell off the bench. 'I mean it, Marv. No. I told you and told you . . .'

'All right,' the boy said angrily. 'So save it until you're ninety. A lot of good it'll do you then.'

The girl straightened her clothing.

'What a square,' the boy said. A match flared as he lit a cigarette. He sat on the bench, slouching forward, dragging on his smoke.

The girl hesitated. 'I'm sorry if I misled . . .'

'Ah, go on. You sound like someone out of ancient history. Twenty years old and still doesn't know what it's all about.'

10

'If you're going to get nasty . . .'

'Go home to Momma,' the boy said bitterly.

The girl turned and walked along the side of the court, back toward the road and the flap in the wire.

'What sort of college is Simmons anyway?' the boy called after her.

The girl walked faster.

'And what about those jokes you told me? Like sleeping on my first Simmons and all that? Talk about being misled!'

Ted crawled away from the fence. He got to his feet and hurried through the grass and through the birches and onto the road. The girl had just passed him, walking toward the turn and the lodge. He brushed at his knees, and she heard him and looked over her shoulder. He said, 'Good evening.' She stopped and peered at him. When he came up close, she said, 'Oh, hi,' and he finally recognized her. She was a waitress who served tables near his.

'Hi,' he said. 'I wonder if you know where I could find the boy who rents out the boats. I'm leaving tomorrow and want to thank him for some special favors.' He paused. 'Like giving me a canoe that doesn't tip too easily when I'm out with a girl.'

She smiled. 'Stan? He's probably down at the dock.'

'At this time of night?'

'He's not working, if that's what you mean.'

She started to walk. He walked beside her. He could smell her perfume and a musky undercurrent. His heart was hammering.

'I should think there are nicer places than a splintery wooden dock to take a girl.'

'Believe me, he's not on the dock.' She laughed. 'You know that room off the side where he keeps the oars? He also keeps two canvas covers there. He's supposed to put them over the beached rowboats when it looks like rain. He doesn't – he uses those covers . . .' She glanced at him.

Ted understood. The boy at the tennis court had insulted her, injured her faith in herself as a woman. Now she was trying to renew that faith by being worldly and daring with this older man.

He was touched by her effort. He wanted to tell her she didn't have to prove anything to anyone. She was a dark,

11

pretty girl with searching eyes and a husky voice. She could hold boys without giving them anything she didn't want to give them. But she didn't know this yet.

At the same time her perfume and musky odor heated his senses, and he fought the desire to ask her to help him, to be good to him – fought the mounting impulse to put his arm around her waist and draw her to him.

He needed her tonight. He needed her as she would never be needed in all her life.

'Just how do I get to the dock?' he asked. 'I'm lost after sundown around here.'

She pointed. 'The path is just ahead, on the left. It goes down to the lake. Rock steps, remember?'

'Well ... would it be asking too much to take me down there?'

She looked at him. He met the look. She dropped her eyes and walked a few more steps. 'All right.'

'My name's Ted.'

'Maureen.'

'How lovely.' And he took her arm, his fingers pressing her bare flesh as they turned toward the birch railing and the path down to the lake. He remembered her face tilted to the sky, pained by desire as the boy pressed kisses to her legs.

The boy had been a fool. He had given up too soon. Maureen wanted love. Maureen's face had reflected how much she wanted love. It was all a matter of making her know she wanted it.

What was it Susan had once said? 'I guess every girl secretly hopes she'll be raped by certain boys. That way she'll get the sex she craves without the self-condemnation, the guilt.'

He wondered if it would take much raping to convince Maureen.

CHAPTER TWO

The boathouse boy was in the storage room, but he [ ] alone. Ted knocked at the door and it opened and then was the boy, looking bleary-eyed and sullen. He smelled of alcohol. 'Yeah?' he said, and then his eyes slid beyond Ted and saw Maureen; the sullenness disappeared. 'Hey, Maureen. Thought you and Marv were on for tonight.'

'We were, Stan, but now we're off.'

'That's too bad.' He grinned, then looked at Ted. 'What can I do for you?' He seemed to be asking Ted to go. He seemed to be saying he wanted a crack at Maureen.

'I'm leaving tomorrow. Thought I'd thank you for your services.' He reached for his wallet, and his hand shook. That hard face. Those hard eyes. That tough, challenging, questioning look – the look on the boy's face that night in November.

'That's darn nice of you,' Stan said, and grinned. And the grin was wrong. The boy hadn't grinned.

Other things were wrong. He knew it ... but Stan was close. He hated anyone close. He handed Stan five dollars.

'Thanks. Now I can drive into town tomorrow night and buy myself a few beers.' He looked past Ted at Maureen. 'Now I can ask someone to come along. That is, if she'll sit down and talk it over with me tonight.'

Stan wore olive-green chinos and a T-shirt. He was too broad. His face was too thick. But still, he was a tough kid with challenging ways.

He stepped past Ted, onto the dock. 'After my friend here leaves, you wanna come in and talk, Maureen?'

Ted said, 'Your friend here is *her* friend for tonight.'

The girl looked at him, surprised. The boathouse boy caught the look and murmured, 'She don't seem to know it.'

'I ... uh, was going back to my room,' Maureen said, but she didn't leave. Marv's insults still rankled, Ted guessed. 'Mr ... Ted asked me to show him the way here.'

'Well,' the boy said, turning to Ted, 'she showed you the way. Thanks and good night.'

'Good night to you,' Ted said, and went to Maureen, took her arm and turned her to the path.

She went along, her smile uncertain. But she glanced back, and Ted knew it was an invitation. Would Stan receive it?

He got his answer as footsteps came up behind him.

'Hey, hold it! Maureen didn't say . . .'

Maureen stopped, but Ted moved her on again. Stan grabbed his arm. Ted let go of Maureen and turned and walked into Stan, pushing him back, leaving Maureen behind and out of the way. 'You're starting to bother me,' he said, the redness engulfing him.

'Yeah?' The boy wasn't at all frightened. He was strong and he was tough and he'd been nipping from a bottle of whiskey. 'If you think your five dollars buys you the right to walk away with one of my friends, you're nuts.'

'Stan, he's a guest!'

'That doesn't enter into it,' Ted said. 'I'll be gone tomorrow, and I don't need the manager's help in handling this punk.'

Stan moved back another step, drew himself together and clenched his fists. 'You watch your big mouth, mister.'

Ted slapped his face. Stan swung his left at Ted's stomach, his right at Ted's chin – classic and easily anticipated. Ted's reaction was automatic and blindingly swift. He moved low and into Stan. His left arm shot up and out, inside Stan's right, causing the boy's punch to go wide. His right side turned into Stan's body, his right arm clamped over Stan's left, his armpit a vise in which the boy was held fast, his right leg hooked behind Stan's left leg. Meanwhile, his left hand had dropped, and he sent it heel-first into Stan's chin. As the boy's head snapped backward, Ted released his arm. The boy went down on his back and hit the dock with a thump.

Maureen cried out. Stan sat up and shook his head and began to get up. Ted stepped in and chopped at the side of his neck, but the boy dodged the wrong way and put his face into the blow. His nose got it. 'Oh, Jesus,' he said, and surprised Ted with a convulsive, grabbing motion. He pulled Ted down, but then he went limp. Ted scrambled over him, not using the opportunity to knee and kick. He got up and

14

turned and saw that Stan was lying still, bleeding heavily.

'Do something,' Maureen said. 'Help him.'

He bent to the boy and used a handkerchief on his nose. Stan groaned and looked at him. 'You dirty bastard,' he said, voice muffled by the handkerchief. 'You fight like an animal.'

Ted smiled and straightened. 'He'll be all right.'

'Are you sure?'

That shamed Stan, who sat up, pressing Ted's handkerchief to his nose. 'If he wasn't leaving tomorrow, I'd show you who's all right and who isn't. I'd fight the same way and then we'd see who got it.'

Ted smiled again. He felt much better now. He went to Maureen. Her face was tight, closed. 'I'm sorry,' he murmured. 'I had no choice.'

She began to walk. He walked with her. They started up the path, and he took her arm. But he didn't concentrate on her until he was sure there was no danger from behind. Then he said. 'Are you angry at me?'

'Does it matter?'

'Yes. I want you to like me.'

'It's all so silly. You're leaving tomorrow.'

'Tonight's more important than tomorrow.'

'Tonight? One night? What can happen ...' She came to a stop as his arm moved around her waist.

He told her she was a beautiful woman. He said he had watched her all week in the dining room, and had wanted to speak to her but hadn't had the nerve.

'I see. You mean you're the shy, introverted type.'

He drew her against him and kissed her. She didn't resist. She didn't help either. He maintained the kiss and caressed her body. She began to push at him. He wanted to beg her, but he fought it back. Susan had walked out on him the one time he had given in to the impulse to beg for love. And that girl Corinne he had picked up in a bar ... he had frightened her so badly she had run from his apartment before he had been able to stop her. He didn't want to frighten Maureen. He couldn't let Maureen run from him.

He let her go. She said, 'This is one night I won't soon forget.' She began to walk.

He took her hand. He pressed her fingers, and after a

15

while she looked at him and smiled a little. They reached the road. She turned toward the lodge, but he stopped her. 'I'd like to talk to you, get to know you so we can see each other in the city.'

She made a cynical face. '*Talk* to me?'

He laughed and bent and kissed her cheek and put his arm back around her waist. She went along with him when he turned away from the lodge. She said, 'By the city you mean New York, don't you?'

He was squeezing her waist, rubbing his leg against hers as they walked. He was also looking for a place off the road, a comfortable place where they could stop. 'Yes.'

'I'm not from New York. I'm from Philadelphia.'

'Just a short drive. We could get together . . .' He saw the stand of birches, remembered the tall grass beyond it and turned suddenly.

She pulled back. 'Where are we going?'

'A spot I know where we can sit down.'

'I don't think . . .'

He took her in his arms. He kissed her, gently at first, then savagely as the redness rose and restraint fled. His hands cupped her rear. She was firm and abundant. He began to murmur, 'Please, Maureen, please, I need . . .'

She stroked his neck and pushed her body into his. He was so grateful tears filled his eyes. Then she murmured, 'Wait. Just one moment. Wait . . .' She detached herself gently, smiled, nodded and stepped back, then ran up the road toward the lodge. She was around the turn and out of sight before he realized she had tricked him.

He stood in the darkness, filled with pain and rage and shame. Trembling, he lit a cigarette and inhaled deeply. It took a while, but he calmed himself, reminded himself that she was young and inexperienced. She had rejected her date at the tennis court and probably rejected all men when they wanted sex. And she and Susan and Corinne were the exceptions rather than the rule in his life. He'd had women, several women since November. Only a month ago he had met Edith Collers and taken her to dinner and gone to her place and she had wanted him so badly she did everything without being asked.

Edith was older than she admitted – at least his age – but

16

she didn't look thirty-six; she took care of herself and wore good clothes and when the clothes came off was an erotic frantic lover. A creative lover.

Myra had been the opposite. Myra had been unwilling to depart from the ordinary. She hadn't been too successful in bed ...

Now he was thinking of what he had sworn not to. Now he was thinking of Myra's failings, of how he had quarreled with her a week before the end, of how he had actually considered a trial separation. But *she* hadn't known it. They had made up and she had thought their marriage was as it had always been (or as it had always appeared to her to be). She had been happy. She had died happy ...

He began walking toward the lodge. Maureen no longer mattered. Nothing mattered except getting from under the tearing, clawing memories. He thought of Dr Carthrage.

Dr Carthrage had explained things to him. No marriage is perfect, Dr Carthrage had said. Statistics prove it, if common sense doesn't. No marriage is perfect, and Ted certainly had nothing to feel guilty about. Nothing real and logical.

Dr Carthrage had made that perfectly plain those first few weeks when Ted had followed Wallace's advice and sought help. Dr Carthrage, or John, as he had asked to be called, had said that after the death of a loved one, the bereaved *searched* for things to feel guilty about. And in the case of a tragedy like Ted's, the guilt was bound to be readily available. 'But all normal. Abnormally normal, one could say, Ted. You've suffered a particularly brutal separation. There will necessarily be mental complications. But a month, two at the most, and basic sanity will reassert itself.'

That was nine months ago. Perhaps the doctor had over-estimated his basic sanity.

The light was on and Wallace was getting into his trousers when Ted opened the door. Wallace dropped to the edge of his bed and sat there, face pale, trousers dangling from one hand – a Buddha in checked blue-and-white drawers.

'Just took a walk,' Ted said, closing the door.

'A walk,' Wallace muttered.

Ted began unbuttoning his shirt.

'Look in the mirror.'

'Listen, I'm tired . . .'

'Look in the mirror. Then tell me whether or not we have to get out of here.'

Ted went to the dresser. His shirt and slacks were splattered with blood. 'Yes, well, there was this rough kid and we had words.'

'Hard words, I'd say.'

Ted smiled and took off his shirt and walked to the bed nearest the door and took off his trousers and got under the covers. 'Turn off the light.'

'You sure they're not going to come looking for you?'

'The kid had a nosebleed.'

Wallace stood up. 'Why'd you have to sneak out tonight, the last night? We discussed the situation frankly, didn't we? You admitted it was best if we stayed together. You said exercise and food and lots of sleep. Was a girl involved?'

'You sound like my keeper instead of my brother-in-law.'

'We discussed the situation and decided . . .'

'This boy resented my being with this girl and said things and we fought and he got a bloody nose. The end.'

'One of the waitresses?'

'Who else here is under sixty?'

'But they're all such kids.'

'Here we go again. Because I'm thirty-six doesn't mean I can't take out a girl in her twenties, does it?'

'But why would you want to when the city is full of mature women?'

Ted had to look at him then. Wallace was a year younger than he was, but looked five years older because of his balding head and short, heavy body. And because of his retreat from everything youthful – clothes and speech and actions. He was going to fat, as Myra had begun to go, and women rarely gave him a second glance.

'You're asking me why I'd want to take out a lovely young girl? You can't think of a single reason?'

Wallace flushed. 'That single reason is more applicable to a mature woman than to a child, a college kid. How would you like it if *your* daughter . . .' He stopped, and his silence

18

was full of pain. 'I'm sorry,' he finally whispered.

Ted said to please turn out the lights and not to wake him for breakfast as he wanted to sleep late; they would leave in the afternoon, if it was all right with Wallace.

In the darkness he fought against thinking of Debbie. His daughter. His nine-year-old who would never be ten, who would never grow into a college girl and go away and meet boys and make love.

A little later he got up and felt his way across the room to the dresser. Wallace said, 'What is it?'

'Nothing.' He opened the bottom drawer, found the fifth of bourbon and took a long drink.

Wallace said, 'Put on the light and use a glass and water, for the love of God.'

He said, 'No,' and belted it down from the bottle, drank until his stomach burned. Then he went back to bed and waited to grow drunk and waited to sleep.

They didn't leave until four. They had a late lunch and Ted looked across the dining room to where Maureen was serving an elderly foursome. She never glanced his way that he could see.

On the road Wallace kept the big Olds station wagon moving at a steady sixty miles per. 'I've been thinking,' he said. 'It seems to me you should start looking for someone to be serious about. I'm Myra's brother, and if *I* can say it ... well, it's time. A wife could be the answer to your problems.'

'I'm seeing someone,' Ted answered, and was surprised at himself. He had wanted to discuss Susan but hadn't thought he would.

Wallace glanced at him, and in spite of what he had just said, his expression was bleak; his eyes seemed to say, 'So soon! Myra, sister, forgotten so soon!'

The fool! Myra was forever. Debbie was forever. Scars on his brain, his heart.

But then Wallace smiled. 'That's good. Tell me about her.'

Ted shook his head. 'Nothing, really. Don't misunderstand. I mean, she doesn't even know. And young, a kid, really. No, just something ... trying to get back ...'

He waved his hand and lapsed into silence. He regretted having mentioned her. Trying to explain how he felt, what Susan meant to him, what he meant to her, he realized he didn't know. It was not to be talked about. Not yet.

'Do I know her?' Wallace asked.

'No.' He was suddenly thirsty. He wanted a beer. No, something stronger than beer.

'Where did you meet?'

'We just passed a sign. There's a tavern up ahead. Would you mind stopping? I'd like a drink.'

Wallace gave him a quick, questioning look. 'We'll get into New York after dark as it is. How about a Coke at a roadside stand?'

'It won't take long. And I don't want a Coke.'

'I should think that last night . . .'

'I need it. Please.'

Wallace muttered, 'Okay,' and then, 'To tell the truth, it's not your drinking that worries me. It's your getting into arguments. If a kid happens to look a little like the one you saw that night . . .'

'I won't raise my eyes from my glass.'

'And it wouldn't be so bad if you fought like other people. You'd get your lumps once in a while and have to give it up. But that judo . . . you'll kill someone someday.'

'Don't be silly.'

'I mean it. A black belt shouldn't go around fighting with people.'

'I'm not a black belt. I never went beyond first *kyu*, or brown belt. I never will.' But he didn't explain that he had added expertise in karate and had practiced this personal jujitsu in areas other than a *dojo*, or gym. 'I'll just have a few drinks to relax and then we'll be on our way.'

The tavern off the highway was nearly empty. They sat at a little table in the bar section and Wallace had a sandwich and beer and Ted had a beer to slake his thirst and then two martinis on the rocks. Martinis always hit him hard. They didn't fail to do so this time. He leaned back with a cigarette and looked around. A man and woman sat at the bar. They were middle-aged and well dressed and good looking. And obviously sick and tired of each other. They drank and quarreled steadily, trying to keep their voices low but drawing weary looks from the bartender every so often. Ted began to listen.

'It's not any *one* thing,' the man said. 'It's an *accumulation* of things. Like throwing out those slacks. How many times have you got rid of clothing I value? How many times have I had to raise hell?'

'Who knew you valued them?' the woman said. She sipped her drink. 'You have a persecution complex. You're a schizo. They were just a pair of torn pants a bum wouldn't wear.'

'But you never *asked* me. And all the other times. Is it schizophrenic to recognize that you have a hidden desire to hurt me, anger me, drive me out of my mind? What about all the other times?'

The woman laughed and turned away. 'Drive you out of your mind? You were born out of your mind. All the other times ... who remembers your imagined persecutions? When we were courting you used to tell me what your mother did to you. Now it's me.'

'The tennis racket. I wanted to restring it. And Joey's bike. All it needed was a few spokes. And that beautiful cut-glass decanter ...'

The woman laughed again, a raging sound. 'The tennis racket! The frame was warped.'

'In *your* opinion. You could at least have discussed it with me.'

'Do you discuss each decision you make at the store with *me*, and *before* you make it? My store is the house. I have to make decisions there just as you ...'

'What about Joey's bike? He cried, didn't he?'

'He cried because you raised such a fuss. He hadn't used it in months. And you hadn't used those pants and racket and five-and-dime decanter in *years*.'

The man beckoned to the bartender and ordered. When the bartender had poured and moved away, he said, 'If you ever use that word schizo again ...'

The woman faced him. 'Yes?' Her voice climbed. 'Yes, you'll do what?'

'When we get home ...'

'One bit of obscenity, one even slightly physical act ...'

21

'And you'll run to Brother John in Cincinnati? Big threat!'

'I'll run to the best suite at the best hotel and you'll pay for it. And you'll pay for everything else you've done in the past sixteen years.'

'Sixteen years,' the man said. 'My God, sixteen years of *this*!'

Ted suddenly stood up. 'Let's go.'

Wallace was pouring the last of his beer. 'What's the matter? I haven't finished, and we've got to get the check.'

'What's the *matter*!' Ted repeated.

Wallace glanced at the bar. 'You mean them?'

Ted sat down again. 'I mean people. All the beautiful people in this beautiful world.'

'Oh, brother,' Wallace muttered. 'And here I was thankful no kids were around.'

Ted didn't answer. He had no quarrel with Wallace. But he wanted out of here. The good martini feeling was slipping away. Tension was taking its place. And the man and the woman went on, using words as razor blades to cut each other to ribbons.

Wallace drained his glass and looked for the waiter. 'They're probably quite happy at home,' he said.

'Ecstatic.'

'That's life. You've got to learn to accept it.'

'Do I? Why can't I spit in its face?'

Wallace located the waiter and beckoned.

'It stinks, even at its best,' Ted said, full of sudden awareness. 'At its worst, it's unbearable.'

'I'll file that away with my collection of useful philosophies.'

The waiter came and Ted insisted on paying. As they walked out, the woman began to cry.

'You were thinking of Myra,' Wallace said. 'You were remembering quarrels and blaming yourself for them. You were feeling guilty and lonely. You were dreading going home to an empty room.'

Ted felt better now that the ugly words, the ugly voices, were left behind. 'I'll file that away with my collection of amateur psychoanalyses.' And then, 'It may shock you, but an empty room isn't all bad.'

'It doesn't shock me. I just don't believe you.'

They reached the Olds and got inside and Ted leaned back and closed his eyes. Wallace drove onto the parkway.

Ted thought of that empty room.

From the complexity of married life with its comings and goings and commitments to children and schools and jobs and other people, he had gone to the stark simplicity of single life with its aloneness, stretches of emptiness and freedom to remain uncommitted to anyone but himself.

Wallace was right. It was pretty bad.

Wallace was also wrong. If it had come about naturally, it could have been pretty good at times.

His eyes stayed closed. The car rocked along.

Later a strange sound woke him and he looked around and it was dark. The sound was rain on the metal roof. He straightened in his seat and lit a cigarette.

'It's letting up,' Wallace said. 'You slept almost three hours. We'll be in the city soon and at your place by nine thirty if the traffic stays thin.'

Ted nodded. He was thinking of Wallace telling Laura about last night. Laura would despise him. That bothered him more than anything right now. Yet he didn't know why. He had nothing at stake with Laura – that dehydrated little woman with cold eyes and sharp voice whom he had known for twelve years and never really looked at.

Wallace had put on the car radio. He found music – popular music in fox-trot tempo – and turned up the volume.

And Ted remembered a night almost thirteen years ago when he *had* looked at Laura, a night before either of them were married and they had liked to switch partners and dance with each other.

He had actually never forgotten; but now it came to the front of his mind and he saw the hotel dining room and the band as he and Laura danced and Myra danced with her brother. Laura had always been lean and small, but not quite dried out during her early twenties. And that night she had worn the right dress, a figure-hugging black thing, and the right hairdo and the right perfume; and he had been drinking the right drink, martinis. He had pressed tight against her, letting her feel his maleness, and she had

23

struggled to pull away. He had laughed and said, 'Am I that bad looking?' She had answered him forthrightly; Laura had always been forthright. 'No. Not bad looking. Just bad.'

She had gone on, but there was no point in recalling every last word. And after that they had seen less of each other. And later it had all been forgotten.

He flipped his cigarette into the rain. He leaned forward and muttered, 'Noisy as hell', and shut off the radio. He was annoyed with himself. Why should he be thinking of Laura now, of any woman now? Outside the car the country was disappearing; the city was making itself felt. Somewhere in the city was the boy. He had to find him, he had to kill him. The police hadn't done anything. Nine months, almost ten – all the dragging days since November – and they hadn't found a thing.

He had given up calling Lieutenant D'Andrea. It was always, 'Nothing yet, Mr Barth. We'll call you – soon as anything breaks.'

He leaned back, shut his eyes and tried to sleep again. He couldn't sleep again. He said, 'I feel as if I've stolen a week from Laura and the kids. A week of your hard-earned vacation.'

'Don't be silly. We're going away in a day or two, if my schedule works out.'

They passed the George Washington Bridge, a string of bluish-white lights over oily blackness. The city grew dense on their left.

'Why don't you go back to that analyst?' Wallace asked abruptly. 'You said he was helpful, yet you quit after two or three visits. You should've kept it up.'

'Don't worry about that,' Ted muttered. 'Worry about your sister's killer. He's loose outside.'

'The police worry about that. I'm not a policeman. You should realize you're not either.'

They left the West Side Highway and drove crosstown, into the heart of Manhattan. The rain had stopped. People moved along the glistening streets.

This was New York, mammoth metropolis on the Hudson ... the ugliest city on earth, Ted felt – the dirtiest and most vicious. It had more drug addicts than any other occidental city; and every addict was a potential thief and

24

killer. And that was what the boy probably was, according to Detective Lieutenant D'Andrea.

'Only a dope addict would pull a hot prowl,' D'Andrea had said. 'Break into an apartment with the occupants on the premises. Only a dope addict would kill a woman and a nine-year-old child without reason. Not for sex or for profit, but merely to shut them up. A dope addict or a maniac.'

'You ought to go back to work,' Wallace said, still lecturing. He drove across First Avenue to the tall, brick building. He parked in front of the small, private entrance, down the block from the canopied lobby entrance. 'It's time you took up your career.'

'Can you see me writing memos, dictating letters, lecturing on drug company public relations? That was my career.'

'You made a damn fine living at it.'

'I needed a damn fine living, then. I don't anymore. I've got some money.'

Wallace was silent.

'All right, Myra's money. Myra's stock. Or the stock her mother left her. It's not my fault you quarreled with your mother and she took it seriously. It's not my fault she didn't leave you an equal share. You want me to sign some over to you?'

Wallace said coldly, 'I wasn't talking of stock. I was talking of jobs. I was talking of building your life around a sensible activity again, not searching for killers like some TV detective or beating up people or doing God-knows-what-else with your life.'

Ted opened the door and got out. As he walked around the front of the car to the sidewalk, Wallace raced the engine. He leaned on Wallace's window and said, 'You've got quite a motive to run me down. If I die now, you get all the stock. My will reads that way.'

Wallace rolled his eyes heavenward. 'I don't care a damn about that money! Or even if that's not quite true, it's *you* I'm trying to straighten out and . . .' He sputtered, unable to articulate his feelings.

'Okay. Bad joke. Give my love to Laura and the kids. Kiss Betsy for me. Ken too, but a special kiss . . .' He stopped, because it was a kiss for Debbie, his sweet, lost Debbie, he wanted to send.

25

They said good night and he watched the Olds drive to the end of the block and turn; then he looked at the canopied entrance, the entrance he and Myra and Debbie had used for seven years, while they had lived in their five-room apartment on the top floor. The management had offered him the groundfloor studio apartment two weeks after the murders. He had accepted. He hadn't been sleeping in the big apartment anyway. He hadn't been able to step inside the door, once the police were finished. It was full of screams. Instead, he had stayed with Wallace and Laura.

He didn't want to think of that. He wanted to feel pleasure – wanted to smile, to laugh. Real laughter. Laughter that came up from the guts and shook a man with delight. Laughter at a funny story or a slapstick movie or something someone you loved did to tickle your insides. He hadn't laughed, not really, in almost ten months. How long could a man live without laughter?

Susan. He had felt laughter close by when Susan drank an ice-cream soda. The cheeks-in, little-girl, sucking face. The self-appreciative grin as she caught his look. He had felt laughter very close.

He would call Susan. It wasn't too late, so she wouldn't be asleep yet. He hurried under the brick archway which led to his room-and-kitchenette apartment.

Her brother Hank answered. 'Hey, Ted, how was the vacation?'

Ted said fine and could he speak to Susan.

'The queen is out.'

He knew it was another date because Hank didn't offer an explanation. Not the movies or shopping or visiting relatives. Just out.

He said tell her I called and so-long and hung up. He thought of her with another man; a young and confident man; a happy, laughing man. He began to walk around the room furnished with rollaway bed and two armchairs and TV set and coffee table and books and dresser and rug. He went to the kitchenette and made a drink. He wanted to go to sleep, but knew he wouldn't.

He knew he would go walking tonight.

CHAPTER THREE

He became aware of the headache quite suddenly – a painful pulling together above the eyes that sent tendrils of nausea deep into his stomach. It was a powerful headache that must have been in the making for quite some time. Perhaps it started back in Wallace's car, perhaps as far back as the tavern off the highway.

He was walking along a dark side street, heading west of Broadway into a neighborhood of tight-packed tenements existing within sight and sound of the theater district. He had reasons for going there – none of them conclusive, but together totaling the only plan he had been able to devise.

The boy had been white, so Harlem and the Puerto Rican districts would make little sense. If he was a narcotics addict, as D'Andrea assumed, statistics indicated he was from a slum district. If he wasn't an addict, the same still held true. (Although an occasional middle-class or upper-class kid went bad, the chances were overwhelming that any boy who robbed or killed was from a poor family.)

Ted had already covered large sections of Little Italy, both uptown and in the Village. He had walked Yorkville and the lower East Side. He had searched the pockets of lower-class neighborhoods isolated by the new apartment-house complexes that were scattered throughout Manhattan. He refused to think of the vastness of Brooklyn and Queens, though he had driven through all five boroughs to check pawnshops for the stolen camera, the transistor tape recorder and Myra's engagement ring.

He knew his chances of finding the boy in a city of eight million were infinitesimal, but that knowledge was rational, and he didn't function rationally now. He was hunting the boy who had broken into his apartment nine months ago; and he would go on hunting for as long as it took – years; all the years of his life, if necessary. He hunted five or six nights a week, and watched continuously – even when he was out with a woman. (No, the boy would not move from the city, would not leave New York and throw the search into the realm of impossibility. No, he would trust in Someone to prevent that. It could not happen.)

His headache was terrible. With each step, the agony intensified. He had to take something. Liquor wouldn't work; he knew *that* from other nights, other headaches. Double doses of aspirin usually failed. And this was one of the worst headaches yet. He needed something strong – something special.

He reached a corner and, seeing two boys, he turned uptown to pass them. They leaned against the wall beside the darkened entrance to a grocery store. Their laughter rose, sharp, cruel and frightening. He came toward them, not turning his head, watching from the corners of his eyes. His heart quickened. One sucked on a cigarette. The small glow illuminated a thin face with a wide mouth and large eyes. The wrong face. The other was in shadows. Ted said, 'Could you tell me the time?' The one smoking raised his wrist. Ted stepped closer, to see the other one. 'Almost eleven. Five minutes to.' Ted saw the other one. Light hair and strong face – a hard, challenging face. His voice shook as he said, 'Thanks.' The boy was close. Maybe ... but his hair was too light. And he was too young – not more than sixteen. But still, close.

He turned away, torn by indecision, even though he knew it wasn't the right boy. He hated anyone that close.

They laughed behind him, and again the sound was cruel and threatening. He wanted to turn and strike – wanted to force the boy to confess. He kept walking. It got harder to keep walking each night.

To make a decision, to kill and be done with it, to say the boy was finished ... How good it would be!

His head throbbed. He saw a neon sign on the next block. A pharmacy. He hurried toward it. A woman crossed in front of him at the corner. She wore a black-and-white print dress, tight across the breast and bottom. She looked at him, cleared her throat and smiled tentatively. A hustler. Not bad looking. Black hair and very pale skin and good legs. Young. But he didn't pause. The search dominated him. Some other time. He waited for a car to pass and crossed the street. He approached the pharmacy ... and felt a sharp pang, a stab of memory. It was a corner shop; one plate-glass window was on the avenue and the other was on the side street like Cohen's in the old neighborhood. It had dusty displays and dirty glass and an air of lost ambition like Cohen's in the old neighborhood. He almost passed it by. He hated to bring up anything from the past, even the far past before Myra and Debbie, before college and the climb upward. It reminded him how well he understood poverty – the same poverty that had led to the boy and the murders. He didn't want to understand the boy. The boy was black and his vengeance white, and that way it was simple; that way he could do something about it.

He had to get something for the headache. It was killing him. He opened the glass-and-wood door, squinting into the brightness of fluorescent lights hanging from a ribbed metal ceiling. There were tables on the left piled with cosmetics and soaps and drugs. On the right were shelves. Ahead was a short counter hemmed in by displays of toothpaste and shaving cream. The druggist sat there, a newspaper open before him. He nodded and said, 'Nice night, now that it's rained.' He was plump and gray-haired, with a warm smile. Cohen had been younger, with a thin moustache and a face that hardly ever smiled as the years went by and his diploma browned and his hopes for success browned, year by year. Ted felt better, seeing that this man was different.

He came to the counter. 'I've got a bad headache. Almost a migraine headache. Can you give me something for it? Aspirin won't do.'

The druggist stood up. He wasn't much taller standing; a really small man. 'Well, there's lots of products. There's the new super aspirins. But I always get good results from Empirin. What do you usually take?'

'I've got a prescription – a sleeping pill, really. It's at home. Empirin's much too weak.'

The druggist went in the back. Ted took out cigarettes, then put them away as nausea tickled his throat. The druggist returned with a prescription jar and a glass of water. He shook out two red-and-white capsules and gave them to Ted. 'Try these.'

Ted took them with water. He reached for the jar. The druggist said, 'No, can't sell them without a prescription.'

Ted put a dollar on the counter and turned away. As he

29

reached the door, the druggist said, 'I wouldn't plan on driving tonight, or trying to do any complicated work. Best thing is to lie down.'

'Walking all right?'

The druggist shrugged.

Ted went out. Cohen had also dispensed drugs like a physician. Druggists in poor neighborhoods had to. If they didn't, the man on the next block would. Poor people couldn't run to the doctor for every minor ailment, no matter how much pain there was. But in the better neighborhoods they demanded a prescription for every little thing, including a diaphragm.

These were the two worlds of every society. Nothing to feel upset about. But he did. He felt threatened. He had to walk the streets of that poor world, and memories threatened him. He had to keep reminding himself he had left that world in his early twenties, had been a successful public relations man even before meeting Myra. Now he had investments that by any standards made him well off, and by poor-world standards made him rich.

He came to the next corner and hesitated. He had been through this section, walking the streets to the West Side Highway and the Hudson. He would walk farther uptown before turning west again. That would bring him into new territory. He would take a section of five blocks and walk it, up and back, west and east, from Broadway to the river and back to Broadway again.

He went on up the avenue. It seemed to have grown warmer. He regretted wearing his suit jacket but didn't take it off to carry it. He needed both hands free. Even if he didn't find the boy, he needed both hands free.

That lesson was reestablished as he turned left and crossed the avenue into a side street, a street of garages and warehouses interrupted by a few incredibly decrepit brownstones. A large shape lurched up and out of a sublevel stairway, coming at Ted from the left. It made thick, wet sounds, some of which were words, both menacing and passionate. Ted heard, 'C'mon, little man, little man.' And then the shape was on him and he understood why a man just shy of six feet, weighing a hundred and seventy pounds, would be called 'little man'. Almost every man would be 'little man'

30

to this derelict. He was a towering hulk, even stooping. His face was long, topped by a wild shock of black hair. That was all Ted had time to note.

One massive hand closed on his shoulder, turning him. The other pressed his chest and moved down. The stench of alcohol and sweat was overpowering. And a voice from the shadows said, 'Don't hurt him, Rand. For Chrissakes, don't mess him up.'

Rand didn't mess him up. Rand fell choking from a sharp larynx chop. Ted jumped back, crouching, waiting for that second man to show.

The huge man fell on his side and rolled, strangling on the pavement. Ted watched the shadows of that sublevel area, glancing at the huge man every few seconds. The huge man vomited and passed out. But he made sounds, breathing sounds. He was lucky. It was difficult to control a chop to the Adam's apple. It was fatal all too often.

The other man didn't show. Ted wanted to see him. Maybe he was young, with brown hair.

He stepped around the huge man and moved slowly to the shadows. He took one step down and said, 'Come out!' He heard something move. He started down. Two steps more and he saw a figure. He stopped. The figure made crying, moaning sounds. 'I wouldn't've done it. Rand's the one. He's always got to find new ones. Last week it was a boy, just a kid, but I never . . .'

Ted jumped aside just in time. The figure lunged forward, striking a foot toward his middle. He felt stone to his right, steadied himself and kicked back as the figure came up. He didn't know what he hit, but it was solid, and it crunched. The figure fell. There was no more crying or moaning.

Ted went down. A man lay propped against a barred window. The door to his right was boarded shut. Near the door was a half-empty jug of wine. The man wore a filthy army shirt with epaulets and shoes without stockings. His pants and underpants were near the jug. He looked fifty, and was probably thirty. He had a terrible bruise on the right side of his face.

Ted went back to the street. Rand was sitting up, rocking in pain. He tried to get to his feet. Ted kicked him lightly in the ribs. Rand sat down again, holding his neck. 'Did you ever try asking?' Ted said. He would have liked to laugh, but it was too ugly for laughter. He walked away, looking back every so often to make sure the big man didn't try again.

He walked all the way to the elevated road that was the West Side Highway, and under it to the piers, ignoring hoarse obscenities from an elderly derelict who was sitting against a stanchion. He walked a block north and turned east again. His headache was gone, but he felt tired; far more tired than he should have felt. Those capsules must have contained considerable depressant.

Approaching Ninth Avenue, he was tempted to sit down on a neat-looking stoop. He pushed on. It was almost twelve and he had miles of walking yet to do.

When he reached Broadway, he went one block uptown and turned west, his feet dragging. Why not rest somewhere for just a moment? The street was dark, and deserted but not ominous. Just half a block away lights blazed. Broadway wouldn't shut down for several hours yet.

He saw the double doorway on his left. It belonged to a vast, windowless building – a theater or warehouse – and had a raised step. He would sit down just long enough to shake the lethargy. A moment . . . five at the most. If he saw anyone coming, he would get up.

He tried to pass the doorway. He told himself he would cut short his search tonight. He would go home and sleep.

He sat down. It felt wonderful. He leaned back against the door and looked around. No one on the black street. Back toward Broadway, people walked, couples, everything normal.

He closed his eyes to rest them a moment. And the moment swallowed him.

CHAPTER FOUR

He awoke to terror! He was being smothered. Something dark was over his face and hands were going through his pockets. Was it Rand? Was he being robbed as prelude to obscene assault?

He drew himself together, knifing his knees up, shooting his hands out in stiff-fingered attack. The dark shape fell aside, cursing. He scrambled over it, continuing along the pavement on hands and toes until he could rise and run. There was a shout and the pounding of feet – two sets of feet. His mind still drugged with sleep, he saw the alley and turned into it, then clenched his fists in self-hatred. What if he had trapped himself?

He kept running. It was a long alley, but it ended. It was a *cul-de-sac* – high walls on all three sides with a metal door directly ahead. The door was locked! He turned, threw himself to the side as a flashlight probed for him, waited gasping for the men to reach him. They stopped, whispered to each other, then moved forward slowly. The flashlight came on again. He shouted, 'I've got a gun!' The light went out instantly, but they kept coming.

He crouched, tensed, steadied himself for the attack that would get him past them.

The footsteps stopped. 'Throw the gun out,' one of the men said. 'We won't warn you again.'

If he answered, they might locate him by the sound of his voice. He waited in silence, but something began to bother him. The way that man had spoken . . .

The flashlight came on, swung toward him, caught him even as he threw himself away. He had no choice now. He lunged toward the light, blinded, shouting. He prayed that they weren't armed.

Something hard gave him a scraping blow across the right side of the head. It knocked him to his knees; then he was struck again with agonizing force on the right shoulder. 'All right,' he said weakly. 'Take my money.'

He was hauled to his feet; the light played into his face.

He was slapped across the mouth, cursed, backhanded on the ear. A voice said, 'Okay, Walt.'

He was spun around, his right arm was jammed up behind his back and he was shoved toward the mouth of the alley. As he stumbled forward, he was kneed in the base of the spine and slapped repeatedly on the back of the head. He would have fallen except for hands which took his left arm.

'I said okay, Walt!'

'You said okay. You didn't get a knee in the guts.' Ted was slapped again, so hard he had to be dragged a few steps. 'Any drunk can kick the bejesus out of us, but if we kick back it's police brutality.' Another slap.

Ted knew then what had bothered him before. That voice! It had held authority. It hadn't whispered, sneaking up on him. It had commanded. Too bad they had left out, 'In the name of the law'.

He laughed, and received another slap.

'I thought I was being robbed,' he said, tasting blood on his lips. 'I'm sorry.'

They reached the street. He was told to lean forward against the wall. He obeyed, and was searched with embarrassing thoroughness. 'Where's that gun?' the one who had slapped him asked.

'I wanted to scare you off. Thugs, I mean. I haven't . . .'

'Look around the alley. See if you can find it.'

'If he'd had a gun,' the other one said, 'would he have jumped us bare-handed? Use your head, Walt.'

Walt said, 'You gonna do it or will I?'

The cop went back into the alley. Ted's arms began to ache. 'I'm going to fall over in a minute,' he said. 'I took two capsules for a bad headache and they knocked me out. I must have fallen asleep . . .'

'Shut up.'

Ted shifted weight. 'Listen, I wasn't drunk. I just dozed off because of those pills. When I woke up, you must have been searching me. I didn't see anything but a dark shape and I panicked. You never said you were officers.'

The other cop came back. 'There's no gun in there. And no place he could've thrown it. Must be ten, twelve stories straight up on all three sides.

Walt said, 'Okay, you. Turn around.'

Ted did, dropping his arms with a groan.

'You're coming in, mister.' Walt was a young, hatchet-faced patrolman with big shoulders and a lean body. 'Assaulting an officer should do for a starter.'

'What were you doing in that doorway?' the other cop asked. He was older, heavier, less intense.

'Said he was tired and stopped and fell asleep. Soon he'll be yelling police brutality.' Walt was already worried.

Ted said, 'No, no, I'm lucky to be alive. You could've shot me when I said I had a gun. No, I'm grateful you didn't take the easy way.'

'That's what he says now,' Walt said. 'But when he sees a lawyer . . . Put that flashlight over here, Frank.'

The older cop played his light on something in Walt's hands. It was a wallet – *his* wallet, Ted realized. They read through the cards and flipped the sheaf of bills. He had about thirty dollars.

'Not even vagrancy,' Walt muttered.

Frank took Walt by the arm and drew him away. They murmured together, and Ted guessed they were deciding whether or not to let him go. The decision went against him.

'Into the car,' Walt said. 'Any movement and we put the cuffs on you.'

He went without protest. He still felt he was lucky, even though his head and shoulder were beginning to throb. Sitting between them, with Walt driving, he said, 'Does either of you know Lieutenant D'Andrea?'

'Where's he at?' Frank asked. 'What precinct?'

'Central Homicide. I think that's what they call it.'

'What do you want with him? He a friend?'

'He knows me. He knows I'm not a drunk or a vagrant. He knows what . . . why I'd be out at night.'

'You're still coming in,' Walt said.

'Yes. But if you'll get in touch with D'Andrea before booking me, it'll save us all a lot of time. I don't want a lawyer.'

'You'll need one,' Walt said, but he glanced at Frank.

Frank said, 'Who's on the desk tonight?'

'Keegan. First bit of luck I've had this week.'

'We'll see,' Frank said to Ted. And a moment later, 'You need a doctor?'

Ted was sure he did, but laughed. 'Hell no. Just a night's sleep.'

'Where'd you meet this guy from Homicide?' Walt asked.

'My home.'

Walt glanced at him. 'I thought that name was familiar. Barth. Ted Barth. Something happen to . . .' He stopped. 'Jesus, do I ever pick 'em! Can you hear the sob sisters now? Sweet Mother Mary! And I'm studying for my sergeant's exam.'

'What?' Frank asked.

'Barth. The woman and kid. About a year ago. Both killed in a hot prowl.'

Frank said, 'That right, Mr Barth?'

Ted nodded.

'I'm sorry,' Frank said.

Ted wondered what D'Andrea would say. The detective had warned him the last time. It had been different then – in a different part of town – but he would know.

'Maybe we can just . . .' he began, and looked from one officer to the other.

'No,' Walt said. 'I'd be wide open then.'

'I'd never say a thing. Besides, *I'm* the one in trouble.'

Walt laughed bitterly. 'He's gotta be kidding. This is New York. In New York you're in trouble only if you've robbed, killed or wear a uniform.'

Frank chuckled. Ted smiled, his lips hurting. Walt said, 'Let's hope this D'Andrea's on duty.'

Detective Lieutenant D'Andrea entered the precinct house at a quarter to three. Ted was sitting on a bench to the right of the desk. Walt and Frank were in back somewhere. Ted began to rise, but D'Andrea went past him and up to the desk. He talked to the officer on duty, jerking his head at Ted several times. The desk man used his phone briefly. Walt and Frank came in through a door behind the desk and all four talked. Then the patrolmen went out the street door, Frank giving Ted a nod. D'Andrea came over to him.

'You're not a very smart man, Mr Barth. You're going to get yourself killed. I warned you the last time.'

'I was just resting in that doorway.'

'What were you resting from?' The lieutenant was a

broad man with a smooth, brown face. His voice was deceptively mild. He had black hair, slicked straight back from a high forehead, and small brown eyes. Ted had seen him wear glasses during the early days of the investigation, and they had given him a middle-aged, scholarly look. He didn't look scholarly now. He looked big and hard. 'The last time you beat up two punks who resented your looking into their car. Were you resting from something like that?'

Ted shook his head. 'Took pills for a headache. They made me sleepy.'

'So why didn't you go home?'

Ted's shoulder throbbed. His lips felt stiff and hot. He was beginning to resent D'Andrea.

'You were looking, weren't you? You were playing detective again.'

'One of us has to!' He met D'Andrea's stare. 'It's been nine, almost ten months.'

D'Andrea frowned and sat down. His manner changed. 'How've you been?'

'All right. Anything new?'

'Maybe.'

'Either there is or there isn't.'

'Then there isn't.'

'Why won't you tell me?'

'Because there's nothing to tell, yet.' He leaned back, rubbing his eyes. 'Damn these late tours of duty.'

Ted waited. D'Andrea said, 'I know how much catching that killer means to you. I won't say anything to give you false hopes. But we're working, and a few things have begun to show promise.'

Ted's heart pounded. 'Like what?'

'Like a folder building up and needing only one piece of concrete evidence to point us in the right direction.'

Again Ted waited.

'But it's nothing until we get that one piece of evidence. And even after that, we'll need more. And only when we get more will I tell you we've got a chance.' He stood up abruptly. 'I'm taking you home, Mr Barth.'

In the unmarked Plymouth Ted listened to police calls. Violence filled the city. Violence and accident and illness. Death.

37

'Don't do it anymore, Mr Barth. Use your head.'

Ted watched the streets. Three youths slouched in a doorway up ahead. One seemed the right type. As they fell behind, Ted fought the impulse to turn and stare and shout for D'Andrea to stop. It didn't escape the detective.

'You go walking around the city, don't you? At night. Looking for that kid. You go to the worst neighborhoods and push your nose where it isn't wanted.'

'A citizen may walk . . .'

'Don't play lawyer with me. I know what you've lost. I've got a wife and two daughters.'

'Yes, you've told me.'

'And I'm telling you that you're going to get killed one night. A fat lot of good that'll do your wife and child.'

'It won't hurt them much either.'

D'Andrea looked at him. 'Maybe I should let them put you away a few months. Maybe a little time in one of our modern, spacious prisons would cool you off.'

Ted looked into doorways and parked cars. The neighborhood was changing. If the boy was on these streets, he was looking for prey.

They reached First Avenue and the apartment house. Ted said, 'Not the main entrance. Right here.'

D'Andrea pulled up in front of the brick archway. 'I'm glad you've got a new place. It would've been better to get away from the neighborhood completely.'

Ted opened the door and stepped out on the road side. A cab flashed by, horn blaring. It was a close call. 'See?' D'Andrea said. 'You never looked. You're careless with your life. Ask me and I'd say you were looking for a way out.'

Ted walked around the front to the sidewalk. 'Thanks for getting me off the hook, Lieutenant.'

'Listen, are you going to give me your word . . .'

'No!' Grayness moved into Ted's face. 'Find the boy. Then I'm through looking. Then maybe I can decide what I want to do with my life.'

The lieutenant leaned on his window. 'Now why should your sickness concern me? I mean, I'm no psychiatrist. I try to do my job and I look out for my own ass. Every man looks out for his own ass.'

'What you're saying is you can't find him, and you hide it by spouting soap-opera platitudes about life being worthwhile.'

D'Andrea's face reddened. 'You can look at it that way, if you want. You can also look at it this way. Suicides roast in hell, and what you're doing is suicide.'

'We go to different churches.'

'I know. But there's always the chance mine has the right story.'

Ted bent forward, raging. 'Talk. Ever since that first day you've given me plenty of talk. But you can't find him.'

The lieutenant began to pull away.

'You'll never find him,' Ted shouted. 'I'll have to do it myself. You know you'll never find . . .'

But the Plymouth was down the street and moving fast.

CHAPTER FIVE

Doctor Gorel had been his family physician, when he'd had a family. Ted hadn't seen him since a month or two before the murders – almost a year.

The doctor X-rayed his shoulder, though he was certain nothing was broken. He complimented Ted on his general condition. 'You're a little thinner, but very tight-muscled. Still taking those judo courses?'

Ted said he worked out every so often.

'I'd like to try it myself. Or at least observe a lesson or two.'

The doctor had said the same thing a year ago. Many people said the same thing. Then, if they did observe a class or two, they decided it was much too violent a sport.

'Where was it again, Ted?'

They sat in the doctor's office. Gorel poised pen over pad.

'The Forty-seventh Street Gym. Thursday nights for the advanced class . . . my class.'

Gorel wrote, nodded, murmured, 'Not this week, but soon.'

Ted took out his wallet. 'Then I can use my right arm normally?'

'You can, though I'd try to rest it a bit. At least until the swelling goes down. And give it some heat.'

Ted paid and rose. Gorel was looking at his file card. 'How're those headaches? Still using that prescription I gave you?'

'Once in a while.'

'Reason I ask is I got a call from Peterson the druggist. He said you'd renewed it four times. That's more than once in a while.'

Ted shrugged.

'I told him not to renew after that last time about two weeks ago.'

'Why would you do that?'

'I wanted to see you. Those pills contain a powerful barbiturate. I wondered . . .' He paused. 'Well, in light of the tragedy . . .'

'It's been nine months, Doctor. I haven't killed myself yet.'

Gorel smiled. 'Peterson can call me if you need any more. I'll tell him okay.'

'Thanks.'

In the reception room the elderly nurse said, 'Nice to see you again, Mr Barth. How are your wife and daughter?'

It seemed as if everyone in the world should have known. He said, 'Didn't the doctor . . .' then nodded and went out.

It was a brilliantly sunny day; heat bounced off the pavement in enervating waves. And it wasn't even noon.

He walked back toward the apartment. He would call Susan. Then he would check pawnshops, camera shops and certain little jewelry stores in the area of Sixth and Seventh avenues. He had covered them before, but stolen objects could be held and sold anytime, as well as resold several times. In the next few weeks he would cover all such establishments in Manhattan and begin to rework the other boroughs. At night there were his walks, and every so often he would rent a car and drive through the streets of Brooklyn, Queens, Staten Island, the Bronx. He had been putting off considering Long Island and Westchester County, but they too would have to be checked. There were slum areas all over.

He had so much to do. So damned much to do!

In the apartment he poured a cold beer, sat down at the little table and picked up the phone. He dialed slowly, carefully, so he wouldn't have to dial over again, and again, and again, as he had so many times since November. That came from not thinking of what he was doing.

The switchboard answered and he said, 'Susan Shore, please.' The ring sounded twice, and Susan said, 'Shore, Public Relations.'

'Hi, Shore. Barth.'

She laughed. 'Hi, Barth.'

'Have fun last night?'

'Yes.' She never dissembled. 'Saw belly dancers.'

'And then?'

'And then I came home and tried to make *my* belly dance.'

'You need an audience for that. You should've called me.'

41

'I had an audience.'

He fought to maintain the light tone. 'And did he approve?'

'No. He laughed his head off. It was Hank.'

'And who was the date?'

'Now you're getting nosey. How do you feel?'

'Like taking you to dinner tonight.'

She hesitated. 'I have to go home and fix something for Hank. If seven thirty's all right . . .'

'It's fine. The Gold Coin on Second Avenue?'

'You and your Chinese food. All right. I'll meet you outside. I hate waiting alone at a table, or feeling someone's waiting alone for me.' Her voice was weak and incredibly sweet to his ears. She spoke quickly, the words running into each other, as if she feared being interrupted. And yet he never interrupted her. He doubted that many men did. 'I'll stand in that doorway, or you stand there if I'm late.'

'Will you recognize me? It's been so long.'

She laughed. 'About a week.'

'Nine days and, by seven thirty, five and a half hours.'

She was still laughing. He loved her laughter – weak, like her voice, and soft. 'The intense-lover bit. Five and a half hours. You just made that up.'

'No.'

There was a moment of silence; then she said, 'I really shouldn't eat all that rice and egg roll and starchy food. I'm fat.'

'You've never been fat.'

'How can you be sure when you've known me only a year?'

'Almost eighteen months. That's when you came to Drizer Chemical, remember?'

'All right. Eighteen months. But I was fat at sixteen and fat at nineteen and just before I came to Drizer I had to go on a strict diet. Now I'm putting on weight again.'

'It's all those boys buying you all those dinners.'

'Then maybe we should skip tonight?'

'I'm not a boy. I'm a man.'

She laughed. 'I have to get back to work.'

He wanted to keep her with him. He forgot the streets and the shops and the search when she was with him. 'Why don't

I pick you up at the office and walk you home and wait while you make Hank's dinner? Then we can go to the restaurant together.'

'No. It inhibits me to have guests around. Hank too.'

'Consider me one of the family.'

' 'Bye for now.' She hung up.

He finished his beer and thought of eighteen months ago when he had first met Susan. She had walked by his office and glanced in and smiled. He hadn't had time to smile back before she was gone, but he had asked his secretary who she was. New girl in the department. Trainee writer. He had introduced himself the next time she had walked by. He had stopped and spoken to her whenever he had occasion to be near the PR bullpen. She had taken to dropping into his office for a chat every so often. He had enjoyed looking at her and listening to her – even then, with his life complete, with his wife and child waiting for him each evening. He had taken her to lunch several times, built a daydream or two around her, and counted her among the more pleasant aspects of working for Drizer Chemical. But nothing more. Not that he wouldn't have liked more. Not that any married man in the shop wouldn't have liked more. But Susan wasn't the married-man's-plaything type. She didn't have to be. Her biggest problem was keeping her social life within reasonable bounds and getting a few hours of sleep each night.

Then came November and a flood of condolence cards from the office. Among them was a typewritten note:

'Please think of all the friends you have, all the people who wish you well. Let me know how you are. Susan.'

He had called her two weeks later. He hadn't been very sane then but he had acted sane for her. He had taken her out for a drink, and as they were leaving the bar, he had asked her to dinner. She had hesitated, understanding he was approaching the process of courtship. But when he had said, 'It's important to me, please,' she had accepted. And she had continued to accept.

That had been the beginning. Acting sane for Susan had helped him to act sane for himself. And then the plan to find

43

the boy. And between Susan and his search, a way of life.

Now he wanted to draw Susan closer to him. It wasn't time for declarations of love, but she was his hope for the future.

(Could there be another wife and another child? Would he wake up one morning and hear a woman call him to breakfast, and open his arms for a little girl asking for Daddy's kisses?)

He left the apartment. He could visit the office. He had yet to visit the office. Cort, his department head, had expected a visit. He owed the man a visit. And he could look in on Susan.

She wouldn't like it. She didn't like to be pressured. It was the cool approach that got Susan. (He wasn't nearly cool enough for her. She excused him because of the tragedy. But she was young. The young didn't allow sympathy to dominate their values for too long, so he would have to compete with the cool kids on an equal basis sooner or later.) At Bennington she had admired Humphrey Bogart's old movies as had most of her contemporaries. Even now she would speak of his celluloid personality as the ideal of manhood ... the ask-for-nothing-take-all approach ... the preknowledge of success with women that meant actual success with women.

He had never felt that preknowledge. She would never know he had never felt that preknowledge. And any man who felt that preknowledge with Susan had better stay out of his way!

The red haze of need to do something was upon him. He walked in a tight, slightly stooped coil, telling himself that it was almost noon and the streets were crowding up and people were bound to bump him, ordering himself not to react with anything but a pardon-me or a that's-all-right smile. He remembered every deadly blow, every swift throw, every agonizing grip he had been taught and had taught himself, in the past six years. He had always been a quick student, an eager and capable *judoka*, but only since November had the element of explosive aggressiveness been added.

He began to get a headache. He entered the first cafeteria he came to and had a sandwich and a glass of milk. The

44

headache receded. He went back to the crowded lunchtime streets.

In the second pawnshop the owner said, 'Got a Nikon thirty-five millimeter just like you want. Here, lemme show you.'

He watched the man come toward him, holding the camera. And it was his camera, had to be his camera. But when he took it in his hands, he couldn't find the chip in the right side of the case where he had dropped it the same day Myra had given it to him. It wasn't his camera. It was another Nikon, one of thousands of Nikons.

Suddenly he was rational. Suddenly he saw how impossible it was to search alone in a city of eight million for one camera and one tape recorder and one ring. And one boy. If the police with their thousands of trained men and informers and scientific methods and modern equipment couldn't find him, how could *he*?

He turned and left the shop as the man was saying, 'Hey, this is the Nikon just like you want,' and went back into the street. Sixth Avenue was jammed with people and with boys – boys with brown hair and hard faces. The world was full of boys with brown hair and hard faces and he didn't know which was the real one and he would never know and he had to know, had to find that boy and rip him apart . . .

He went into a bar and had a martini on the rocks and then a beer and then another martini on the rocks. He drank and watched baseball on television. He said the Mets would make the first division in two seasons. The man next to him, heavyset and balding, turned on his stool and stared. 'You some kind of nut?'

Ted laughed. 'No, just a believer in miracles.'

The man explained why it couldn't happen. Ted explained why it could happen, and then he went outside and squinted in the sunlight and headed for the next pawnshop.

He returned to the apartment at six, damp and exhausted. He finally remembered to check the mail. The box was crammed with a week's deliveries. Most was junk and he tossed it away. But there were two dividend checks from two blocks of blue-chip stock, and these he tucked into his wallet. The dividends came in regularly. They averaged between seventy-five and eighty-five hundred a year. When he

45

had been working, that had made up less than a quarter of his income. Now it was his total income, and he hadn't yet touched his cash savings. He didn't seem to need any more than eight thousand. He didn't think he would as long as he remained single.

He showered and shaved for the second time that day, and put on his olive Dacron-and-cotton suit. He began to feel tense, and made himself a small bourbon and water. He wanted another but decided against it. He chewed a piece of chlorophyl gum and watched television until it was time to go.

CHAPTER SIX

He was hungry and enjoyed the food, eating part of Susan's meal as well as his own. She ate lightly. She did seem a little heavier than when he had last seen her.

'How much did you gain?' he asked.

She wore a sleeveless blue-and-white print dress and a blue scarf of silklike material across her shoulders. As soon as they had met, she had informed him the scarf was 'camouflage' for the weight of her upper arms.

'Let's not discuss it,' she said, grinding out her cigarette. She immediately lit another. She wasn't in the best of moods, and for once wasn't bothering to hide it from him. (He had been expecting the end of his special treatment. This might be it.)

He finished a cup of tea and looked around the restaurant. It was small, pleasantly lighted, not too crowded tonight. He had always been happy with the food and service.

'About seven pounds,' she said.

'In nine or ten days?'

'I meant since I stopped watching myself. About a month.'

'I didn't notice it before.'

'And now you do?' She didn't wait for an answer. 'Those last two or three pounds are the ones that show on me.'

She was a big girl, his height in high heels, wide in the shoulders and deep in the chest, with good legs. She had a long face. Her eyes were almost always underscored with fatigue; that was her social life. Her hair was light brown, sometimes blond if he saw her after a rinse. Her chin was narrow without being delicate. Her mouth belonged to a much smaller woman. It was fragile, vulnerable. She did things with her mouth when she talked or smoked or just sat. She moved it around, pursing and pulling to one side or the other – a nervous business, but charming to him. She often started to smile and then the smile slipped away into one of those nervous pulls.

He poured her some tea. She shook her head. 'You haven't even tasted it,' he said. She picked up the little cup and drank for him. She drank like an infant. She sucked at the tea, her cheeks drawing in. He leaned forward, smiling. She put down the cup. 'Arthur hates the way I drink. He hates the way I move my mouth.'

His pleasure came to a sudden end. 'Arthur?'

'A boy I've been seeing. Hank brought him home one night from Columbia.'

'Hank's classmates are a little young for you, aren't they?'

'He's a graduate student.'

'I see.' He waited for her to say more. She didn't. 'What do you care what Hank's friends think?'

'A girl has to care what her dates think of her. He cares what I think of him.'

'Then you've dated him? He was the one who took you to see the belly dancers?'

'Yes. I've been seeing him for several months now.' Her voice had sharpened, grown waspish. 'Though I don't see why I have to give you a full report.'

'You don't. We were talking about the way you move your mouth. The beautiful way you move your mouth.'

'It's ugly. Psychotics twitching and talking to themselves move their mouths that way. Children and recessives drink that way.'

He began to suffer. He wanted to tell her to stop, wanted to beg her to be kind to him, to let him touch her, finally let him love her . . .

He took hold of himself. 'It's too beautiful for run-of-the-mill people.'

She looked away.

The waiter came with the bill. He paid and rose. 'Like to come to my place for a drink?'

'We tried that once.' She was still waspish, preoccupied with other thoughts. He was afraid they were concerned with the new boy, Arthur.

'I may have been a little too ardent that time. I promise not to be this time.'

They came out into the street. It was twilight, a flattering time for the ugly city. In an hour it would be full night and the jungle would begin to howl. Then D'Andrea's radio would crackle with calls. Assault. Rape. Riot. Robbery. Murder . . .

'Aren't you going to answer me?' she said.

'I'm sorry.'

'I asked if you would mind ending the evening early. I'm tired.'

He had to turn away . . . the urge to beg, to weep, to reach out and take her in his arms was so strong. But that would finish everything with Susan. He just had to accept that she was having a bad night.

'No cabs,' she said as he began to hail one. 'Not until you're working again.'

'Then you'll continue to see me?' he asked, voice unsteady.

Her hand touched his arm. He quickly put his own hand over it. 'I'm not being very nice,' she said. 'I'm sorry. Why shouldn't we see each other?'

They walked uptown to a bus stop. He had to ask. 'Is it that boy, Arthur?'

She took her hand away. 'Maybe.' Her voice was sharp again.

'You're not in love with him, are you?'

She made a sound of exasperation. 'Now really, Ted!'

He was afraid he had his answer. But later, outside her street-level apartment in the reconditioned brownstone, she took his hand and led him into the shadows of the stoop. He felt the warmth of her body and cautiously drew her to him. Her arms went around his neck. He sighed, a thirsty man about to drink, and bent to her lips. The kiss was only the third one of their relationship and by far the most intimate. His hand pressed her bottom; her lips parted; he tasted the sweetness of her tongue. Words surged up from his chest — words of adoration, of desire, of need. But he fought them all back down. Susan was already detaching herself. She had given him a sign of her continued interest. She had told him there was hope. He had to be content with that.

'Susan,' he whispered.

She touched his cheek and turned to the door.

'Saturday night?' he asked, still whispering.

She hesitated. 'Phone me Thursday.'

He knew what that meant. She was hoping for Arthur.

'If not Saturday,' she said. 'Sunday would be all right. We could drive somewhere, if the weather is nice.'

He nodded. 'We can do that even if we go out Saturday.'

'Well, we'll see.' She was sharp-voiced again. 'Good night, Ted.'

She bent to put her key in the door. Her bottom pushed out at him, and he turned away from his lust – intense lust with a wild, red undercurrent. If Arthur fondled that bottom, mounted that bottom, he would kill him.

The redness persisted as he walked from the Eighties to the Fifties and his apartment; and he raged at having this new agony to contend with.

Now he not only had to search the streets for the boy and the shops for what the boy had stolen, but he had to watch Susan and find out exactly what this Arthur was doing.

He drank two straight bourbons and got ready to leave for the streets. The phone rang. It was his sister-in-law, Laura. His mind cleared of all redness and his voice grew quiet, anxious.

'I thought Wallace was taking you and the kids away for a week.'

'We're leaving Friday or Saturday. If we really like the place, we'll stay ten or twelve days. That's one advantage of being your own boss. You can extend your vacation, within limits.'

'Sounds good. Where're you going?'

'Amagansett, near Montauk Point. Wallace can get in some deep-sea fishing and the kids can swim in the bay.'

'And you?'

'You know me. A book and an hour of sun is as much activity as I can take.'

He laughed as if it were the brightest, funniest thing he had ever heard.

'Our going away is the reason I called, Ted. I want you to come for dinner tomorrow night.'

He didn't want to go. 'Well, I've accepted another invitation . . .'

'Wallace told me the sort of invitations you've been accepting, and giving.' She laughed – a dry, disapproving little laugh – and he visualized her narrow face and sour mouth. 'We're worried about you. We're all the family you have, and we won't let you go to hell with yourself, if you'll pardon my language. Women are one thing, but violence . . .

Besides, Ken and Betsy want to see their uncle. I'm making your favorite dish – curried shrimp. At least Myra used to say it was your favorite.'

'All right,' he said, and felt depressed about it.

'Wallace'll pick you up on his way home. About five thirty, quarter to six, depending on the traffic. Don't dress up like the last time. You're eating in your own home, with your own family. Now say hello to Betsy. She's standing here tugging at my skirt.'

He braced himself. The high voice, so familiar, so very much like another high voice, said, 'Hello, Uncle Ted. You coming over tomorrow?'

He said yes, his mouth dry. 'And I'll have a surprise for you.'

'A surprise! Is it a Tina Doll like Debbie . . .'

Laura must have covered the mouthpiece and shushed her. When she came back on, Betsy said, under restraint, 'Thank you.' And bursting free again, 'I can hardly wait! I'll tell Ken. He can hardly wait too! 'Bye!'

Laura said, 'Kids. Well, even facing up to what you might hear from *them* is curative. It's almost ten months. It's time to face a lot of things.'

He had to clear his throat. 'See you tomorrow.'

'The child didn't upset you, did she, Ted?'

'No, of course not.'

'Am I pushing too hard?' She was worried now, and for some reason this made him feel better.

'Don't be silly, sister-in-law.'

'Because I wouldn't do anything to hurt you. You know that. I may not show it, but I know what . . . I felt more . . .'

'Tomorrow,' he said, and hung up.

Susan had begun to judge him for himself and not as a man struck by tragedy. He had been waiting for Laura to do the same – and dreading it.

But why dread it? Once again he tried to solve the problem of Laura, for it was a problem; she created anxiety for him. And once again he turned away from it. He went to the streets.

At eleven o'clock, after covering only half a dozen slum blocks, he grasped an opportunity to escape the search.

51

The two girls came by as he was crossing a broad, brightly lighted street. He skipped such streets, at least this far east. The boy wasn't likely to be prowling here.

The girls were young, slender, dressed in quiet browns and grays – a far cry from the obvious hustler he had seen last night. But the style of their skirts and mannish blouses were anything but quiet; they were body molding and revealing.

They were both beautiful: the pale, pale colored girl with the neck-length dark hair and the slightly taller white girl with the frosted bouffant. They both carried large, black leather bags.

He had to turn and follow them. He wasn't sure, but there was something in the way they walked, the way they moved their bodies.

They strolled along, hands just touching. They laughed continuously, glancing at each other and then around, but not at anyone or anything. Their eyes slid by people and objects and their little teeth flashed and their laughter filled the immediate space around them.

He started to pass them. They wore ballerina shoes and no makeup, at least not the kind most girls wear – the obvious kind, the standard kind. But as he came by them, close, he saw they had pale pancake smoothing and whitening their skin, and midnight black underscoring their eyes and clean, dark curves for eyebrows and white, not red, lipstick. They were heartcatching! They were beautiful! He wanted to turn and speak to them – wanted to beg to be allowed to go with them. He needed them tonight.

They began to sing softly. One glanced at him as he passed. Their song was punctuated by laughter:

'Why can't we two get together,
When we do it's balmy weather,
Why can't we two get together,
Baby?'

He hoped that was the tip-off. He slowed and let them come up even with him and said, 'That should be, why can't we *three* get together.'

'Hi,' the colored one said, her smile a moist ripeness.

He moved over toward a lighted display window. They

52

came with him. 'Hi,' he said. The white girl hunched her shoulders a little and looked around and said, 'Hi too.'

Her movement showed how heavy she was in the breast, surprisingly heavy for a slim girl.

'What you said before,' the white girl said, looking him right in the eye. 'That's a good idea.'

'I've got an apartment not too far from here.'

'Great,' the colored girl said. 'The tourists with the hotels bug us.'

'You understand,' the white girl said, 'Maxine and I are a team.'

'Oh yes,' he said. 'I think of you that way.'

The white girl gave him a hard look. The colored girl laughed and took his arm. 'He's sweet, Odine.'

The white girl shrugged, and again the heaviness showed. She looked him over. He was still wearing his good suit. She moved closer. He stood with his back to the window, hemmed in by sweet-smelling women. He trembled with need. 'It's usually fifty each,' the white girl said.

He smiled.

'But for a weekday night, deadsville, and since you got an apartment, well, twenty-five each.'

He kept smiling. 'You don't have to stay too long. An hour or two.'

'How much then?' the white girl asked, eyes narrowing.

He enjoyed the haggling. 'Thirty, for both.'

'Now honey . . .'

'And drinks and sandwiches and television and whatever else you can find.'

The white girl began to argue, but the colored girl said, 'Odine, I need some fast. It's either this or back to the room.' They looked at each other and the white girl said, 'Okay, Mister, you're in luck.'

After they had looked around the apartment, the white girl, Odine, went into the bathroom with her black bag. The colored girl, Maxine, stood near the door, examining his book shelves. He went to the kitchenette and mixed three big drinks and stood there with his jacket and tie on, feeling like a stranger in his own home.

The white girl came out of the bathroom, walked up to him and took a glass. She wore lacy black panties and very

53

high heels, that she must have had in her bag, and nothing else. Just as in good pornographic movies, he thought, where they don't rush the coupling of stark naked men and women. Her breasts seemed enormous, with very wide brown rings at the nipples. She was altogether larger than he had thought.

He said, 'Would you mind turning around?'

She stepped away and pivoted smoothly in model fashion, pulling her pants down on her thighs. 'This is what you mean, isn't it?'

She had long, full, smooth buttocks. 'How very beautiful,' he whispered. He gulped his drink and went to the sleeper couch and opened it. He arranged the pillows and bedding and turned. Odine was pulling her pants back up. 'I think you should pay now.'

The colored girl came across the room and behind him, put her arms around his waist and kissed his neck. 'Make it forty bucks, baby, please. We're worth it and we've got expenses you never dreamed of.'

'All right,' he said, looking at Odine's breasts. He took out his wallet and didn't have enough. He went to the dresser and dug into the shirt drawer and came out with the locked money box. He used the small key on his ring and unlocked the box. He took out a twenty and added the twenty from his wallet, then locked the box and put it away. Odine came to him, took the money and shook her shoulders so her breasts bounced. 'Great little persuaders, aren't they?'

He reached for her.

'The man wants to swing,' Odine said, squirming away. She went to the bed and lay down. 'Why don't you come take off my pants?'

He went to her, and glanced at the colored girl. 'Why don't you join us?'

'You're a doll,' the colored girl said. 'Really, a doll. It's a pleasure to make a doll. Just let me step in the john a minute.'

He went to the bed and took off Odine's pants and Odine took off his pants and after a while Maxine joined them. They were truly erotic girls. They seemed to get drunk, though they'd had no more than that one whiskey.

Later he left them and went to the bathroom and saw the two big purses on the floor. He ignored them until something glittered at the bottom of the toilet bowl. He bent for a closer look. It was an ampule – an empty plastic ampule.

He turned to the bags and opened one. Right on top was a hypodermic needle. In the other bag the needle was in a zipper side-pocket, neatly wrapped in tissue paper along with two more plastic ampules.

That's what Maxine had meant by, 'I need some fast.'

He closed the bags, washed his hands and went back to the studio room. Odine was just lying down. He looked at the dresser. She said, 'Hey, baby, c'mere.'

He went to her. She reached under his shorts. When she saw it was no good, she said, 'Baby's tired?'

He began to get up.

She said, 'Wait, you wanna see something special?' She put her arm around Maxine's waist, her hand searching. The colored girl had dozed off, lying on her side, her back to Odine. She stirred and murmured, 'Mmmm, baby.' Odine kissed her between the shoulder blades. Maxine said, 'That's quite a man,' and turned and came fully awake. 'Hey, Odine, you must be bombed out of your mind.'

'Baby wants to see it,' Odine murmured, and kissed her on the lips.

At first Maxine seemed embarrassed, reticent; then she began working with her partner. Ted could see that this was where their hearts lay. As their murmurings and movements increased, he went to the dresser and looked under the shirts. The cash box was gone. He returned to the bed and reached under the pillow; neither Odine nor Maxine paid him the slightest attention. The box was there as well as the forty dollars. He left the forty and put the box back in the dresser. Then he sat down in an armchair to watch.

It was almost three when he asked them to leave. Odine had gone to the bathroom a second time and sat fully dressed in an armchair, face flaccid, eyes glassy. Maxine picked up her dress and, chattering gaily about getting together real soon, tried to slip the cashbox from under the pillow to her bundle of clothes. But there was no cashbox under the pillow, and she grew abusive. 'How'd you like me to bring your neighbors running with one big yell?'

'Better hide the needle and narcotics first. It could get you a long stretch and cold turkey.'

She stamped off to the bathroom, her sweet bottom jouncing angrily. She came out again, dressed and holding a four-inch switchblade. Behind her Odine blinked stupidly in the armchair.

'Now you better make up the rest of what you owe, mister. That was fifty each Odine asked for the first time. That's our price.'

He wanted her. He hadn't really had her. Odine had been the hungry one. He wanted that beautiful *café-au-lait* girl, and cautioned himself not to damage her too much. She came toward him, catlike. He made himself look frightened, but she didn't even know enough to hold the knife properly: low, to sweep in from the side at his belly. She raised it high above her head.

He stepped in swiftly, applied a wristlock, danced her around, threw her with a foot hooked high behind her right leg. She landed neatly on the bed, and he on top of her. He closed the knife and put it under the pillow.

He didn't bother to undress her. He enjoyed her fight. He hurt her a bit without drawing blood. She wept, begging Odine to 'Hit him with something. Get a knife from the kitchen and stick the bastard!' But Odine sat with head nodding somnolently, muttering, 'That's the way.'

After putting them out, he showered and ate a sandwich while watching the *Late, Late Show*. He felt empty.

There was some sentimental nonsense about a little boy on the TV movie. He was orphaned and living with heartless relatives and ran away and talked in precocious Hollywood fashion about needing 'love to stay alive'. Ted turned it off. It offended his taste and intelligence, and tears pushed at his eyes.

He lay in bed, thinking of all the people sticking needles in their arms, and needing more and more money, and only a few of the women being able to earn that money with their bodies. The others went out hunting.

He dreamed he was asleep and couldn't wake up and a lake of blood was rising about his bed. Debbie was crying for her Tina Doll.

CHAPTER SEVEN

It had been a brutally hot day in the city. It was a brutally hot night in Valley Stream, Long Island, where Laura and Wallace Stegman lived. Their house was large, brick, ranch-type, on a small, grassy plot, one of thirty on the wide, curved street and differing only in color of brick and size of garage. Ted kept drinking beer and perspiring and blaming his discomfort on the trip from the city and the hot curried shrimp ... 'Though it's the best curry I've ever had, bar none, so help me, Laura.' Laura pointed out that the house was air-conditioned to a pleasant 70 degrees and that even the kids had eaten the curry without feeling any heat. He laughed and leaned across the table and patted her hand. 'Then it must be the company.'

She raised her eyebrows. 'Took you thirteen years to respond. Either I'm growing more desirable or you're giving me the business. And I don't think I'm growing more desirable.'

Both Ted and Wallace protested, but she stood up and began removing dishes. 'Yeah, yeah,' she said drily. 'The one thing I'm not is a fool. If a woman is making Ted sweat, it's one in his mind.'

Wallace shrugged and said no one had ever gotten away with complimenting Laura and asked Ted if he would like a good cigar. Ted accepted and they went into the living room where the kids were watching television, having been fed earlier. Betsy jumped up and ran to Ted and threw her arms around his waist. He bent to her and kissed her, and the smell of a girl child – the delicate scent of hair and skin so unlike a woman's, so unique, so painful to memory – caused him to straighten and say, 'It's time I brought in their presents, wouldn't you say, Wallace?'

'Well, Betsy's, certainly, but Mr Kenneth there, I don't know. He didn't act very nice at dinner, according to his mother, and he hasn't paid much attention to his uncle.'

Ken, who had been transfixed by a Western, leaped up from the carpet and screamed, 'That's not fair! Mommy said to let Uncle Ted eat in peace. And I didn't start up at dinner. It was Betsy. She whispered ...'

'Don't you lie about me, Ken! I never whispered!'

'Shit-head, you whispered! Shit-head! You call me shit-head all ...'

'Oooh, you liar!' She was already crying, her round face twisted with anger. 'I never said anything like ... that!' She whirled to Ted. 'Honest, Uncle Ted. I never say things like that. He knows all those dirty words. Worse! He says them and then he says I say them. I say knuckle-head, like Daddy, or idiot sometimes when he's real mean. But he's ...'

'Shit-head,' Ken shouted. 'You said shit-head.'

Wallace made a choking sound. Ted looked and saw he was smothering laughter in his handkerchief. Ken took his cue from that and pranced about shouting, 'Shit-head.' Betsy stood crying, trying to make herself heard.

Suddenly Ted felt a terrible anger and turned from them, wanting to strike that little boy. His head began to ache. He said, 'Wallace, I don't think Betsy ...'

Wallace choked into his handkerchief and muttered, 'Course not. She never ...' and choked some more.

Laura came in. 'Ken,' she said, voice cold.

Ken stopped shouting. 'I was just ...'

'Come here.'

The boy, lean and fair and utterly different from his father and sister, walked slowly across the room. He began to cry even before Laura slapped his face and told him to go to his room. Wallace said, 'Do you think that was necessary?'

'As law and its enforcement is necessary,' she replied, cold and competent as ever. (Ted wondered if she changed in bed with Wallace. She had to; otherwise it would be impossible even to hold her hand.) 'As a set of values is necessary – rules by which to live. As maintaining that there is a right and a wrong is necessary.' Her eyes seemed to touch Ted then, and he felt a chill. 'As teaching Ken that he's responsible for others as well as himself is necessary. As teaching Betsy ...'

'All right already!' Wallace bellowed, raising both hands above his head. 'Chief Justice Laura of the Valley Stream Supreme Court! My God, she never just *makes* her point, she blasts it into Mount Rushmore!'

Laura smiled faintly and returned to the kitchen. Ted went out to the garage to get the presents from the wagon. He still felt that chill. And he was angry at himself. Laura was a fine wife and mother, but what did that have to do with him? He wanted her neither as a woman nor as a friend.

Or was that quite true – the friend part?

There was some sort of contradiction involved. When he was with her or speaking to her, he always strived to make her like him. When he wasn't with her, he vowed never to see her again.

He was sorry he hadn't brought a present for Laura, specifically for Laura, instead of wine for the table. Flowers, perhaps . . .

And immediately he said to himself, 'See? You're doing it again. Crawling in front of that dried-out little woman. She's nothing to you, so why?'

That silly incident almost thirteen years ago? That nonsense when they were dancing and he had been high and she had been puritanical? That moment which had been unimportant at the time and was totally forgotten by her now?

He took the packages from the Olds and walked back through the playroom, still angry at himself. Was he trying to make Laura change an opinion she had held of him for half an hour, thirteen years ago?

He went up the four steps to the kitchen. Laura was just closing the dishwasher.

'Think you might allow Ken to come out and get his present?'

'Of course,' she said, touching his arm with wet fingers. 'Do you think I'm some sort of monster?' Smiling, she went to get her son.

He gave Betsy the three-foot-high Tina Doll and she squealed and hugged it and kissed Ted over and over. 'Just like Debbie's! Ooh, we could put them together and they would be sisters . . .' She talked and played as Laura and Wallace looked on in pained silence and Ted smiled rigidly. Ken insisted that Ted put on a pair of the boxing gloves that were his present. They sparred a little and Ken swung for a knockout and Ted tapped him on the head, making him sit down. It eased the tension and made everyone laugh.

He pleaded an early-morning appointment and Wallace drove him back to Manhattan at ten. 'You're looking a little peaked,' Wallace said. 'I told Laura I wasn't so sure that your seeing the kids . . . Betsy, really . . .'

'You're right. I'm not ready for it. There are memories and all sorts of . . . well, you yourself said it last Sunday at the tavern. Guilt feelings.'

'That's one thing you shouldn't allow, Ted. Remember what that analyst said?'

'Yes. He explained it was normal. I know I did nothing more than other husbands insofar as quarreling and wanting another woman once in a while and . . . you know.'

'Of course not. You were a damn good husband. Myra said so more than once.'

'I know we had many good days together, and only a few bad ones, but I can't seem to remember anything but the bad.'

'Because it ended as it did,' Wallace said, stopping to pay the toll at the Midtown Tunnel. 'I remember once we were talking about our marriages, Sis and I, and she said . . . not the exact words, mind you, but close. She said, "I never thought it would turn out so well. I'm a cold fish, Wallace, but Ted's made me happier than I have a right to be." I asked her if she meant she didn't like going to bed, and she got embarrassed and said . . . again, I can't swear for the words, "I didn't, but Ted's patience and love are changing all that. I owe him so much." I believed her when she said she was a cold fish. You didn't know our mother. Her acceptance of sex was limited to those times she was trying for children. She made it clear that at all other times she considered it something dirty that men did and women endured. And Myra was close to her. Extremely close, right through her teens.'

'You think she was really happy with me?'

'Very. You must have known it.'

'I knew it then. I can't seem to remember it now.'

'You couldn't have forgotten how proud she was of your good qualities. Like the time we were talking of money and she said you refused to touch any of the stock Mom left her. I don't mind telling you it was a sore point with me then . . .'

'It'll be yours some day. Just let me pull myself together . . .'

'Now cut that out,' Wallace snapped, face flushing. 'I said it was a sore point with me *then*. It's over now. Mom wanted Myra and Myra's family to have it. You're Myra's family. I'm doing very well. I don't need it.'

They were quiet for a while. Wallace cleared his throat. 'Anyway, she said you insisted that the stock be left intact, and that it be shared some day by your children and mine. I was touched. I think that's when I started feeling like a bastard for thinking about that stock, and stopped thinking about it.'

'I made enough anyway,' Ted murmured.

'You certainly did. Twenty-five thousand is more than "enough". I must've bragged about you to half . . .'

'But did she say anything more about our *personal* life?'

'Of course she did. Many times. Once when she brought Debbie over to play with Betsy, she said you were a wonderful father. No . . . She used the word *exceptional*. An exceptional father, she said. And that Debbie was wild about you.'

Ted wanted him to stop now. There was an ache building up inside him, and tears and wailings.

Wallace was saying that Debbie had been a happy little girl and they should remember her that way. 'She never knew real pain, real sorrow, Ted. How many adults can say that? Her life was one long day of joy and love . . .'

'All right,' Ted said, shivering, as if August had gone and winter taken its place. 'All right.'

Wallace gave him a worried look. As they approached the house he said, 'Don't think I'm a broken record, but won't you consider seeing Dr Carthrage again?'

Ted said he would think about it. They parked and he got out. 'So long,' Wallace said, and drove away.

'*Goodbye*,' Ted murmured.

He showered and changed into fresh slacks and a polo shirt. He called Susan. He held the phone and listened to the ring at the other end. There was no answer. He dialed again, hoping he had made a mistake, and listened to the ring sound over and over. It was his voice, pleading with her to be there. But she wasn't.

61

The name Arthur seared his brain. Arthur, dancing with her. Arthur, holding her in his arms. Arthur . . .

Or were they in the apartment alone, linked together in passion, ignoring the phone, ignoring his call? Were they laughing there together in darkness rich with the odor of Susan's body, laughing and loving while he cried out for her? Was she saying, 'That's only Ted, Arthur. Pay no attention, Arthur. Arthur . . .'

He got up, still holding the phone, and shouted into it. 'If you are, you are!'

The ring sounded, and behind it he thought he heard laughter. He knew that was impossible, and pressed the handset to his ear and was *sure* he heard laughter. He flung it to the floor and the base of the phone fell too and he kicked it. 'If you are!'

CHAPTER EIGHT

He stood across the street from Susan's place, in the shadows of an alley between two large apartment houses. He couldn't hide himself completely because a padlocked gate blocked the alley. He had been there since eleven o'clock and had received glances from half a dozen passersby. One woman had looked back at him suspiciously as she entered an apartment house farther east, and a moment later a man wearing a porter's cap had come out. Ted had left, heading west, and had gone completely around the block. He had done that three times in the past two hours to avoid groups of pedestrians. Now it was one thirty. Now he was tortured by the thought that if they were inside, neither would emerge until morning. Or if they were somewhere else, Susan wouldn't return at all.

At that moment he saw them, Susan and a tall man, coming around the corner of Second Avenue, walking east toward the brownstone. Even if he hadn't recognized her instantly, her laugh would have told him who she was. It had never sounded softer, sweeter, happier. She looked up at the tall man – a boy, really – now that they passed under a lamppost. A boy of twenty-five or so with thick, brown hair and a big, handsome face and the long, smooth stride of an athlete. There wasn't a trace of cheap swagger in him – just an indefinable air of Ivy League certainty.

Ted's heart sank. This was the toughest sort of competition.

They reached the brownstone, Susan holding to the boy's arm. They talked. Susan laughed. They stepped into the shadows of the stoop. Ted could make out the pale blur of Susan's yellow dress. The boy was a darkness – a darkness in the shadows and a darkness in Ted's heart.

They stayed in there for what seemed like an hour. Then the boy emerged and started to walk away. Susan called, 'Arthur.' The boy stopped. Susan came out of the shadows and laughed and used something to wipe the boy's mouth. Ted quickly told himself that girls kissed even their most casual dates good night, and that nothing had changed, even though this was Arthur and Arthur was handsome. No, she was going to see *Ted* Saturday night . . . if Arthur didn't ask by tomorrow. She was going to see *Ted* Sunday afternoon, no matter what Arthur did. Arthur was a college kid, out for fun. So let him have his fun. Once he realized Susan was serious, he would drop her fast. And Ted would be there, waiting. So everything was all right.

The boy was walking toward Second Avenue and Susan was lingering on the street, looking after him. Ted wanted her to leave so he could go after the boy.

But why go after the boy if everything was all right?

Because everything wasn't all right as long as she could look after a boy that way – a boy named Arthur whom she had felt compelled to talk about when at dinner with another man.

Susan went into the shadows; her door opened and closed. Ted left the alley and walked toward Second Avenue. He crossed the street near the corner and saw Arthur half a block up ahead. He walked faster. Arthur didn't know who he was. Arthur would get into an argument with a stranger and be badly hurt. So badly hurt that a month or more of Saturdays would pass before he would be able to date Susan. And by then Susan would know Ted loved her, and would see her future with him.

He was catching up to the boy. He slowed as he crossed 83rd Street, planning to reach him at the next intersection. That way they could fight on the side street with less chance of being seen and interrupted. Not that anyone was in sight. A lighted bar a block ahead; an occasional cab: a rare private car. That was all.

He planned his move: to bump the boy, to accuse him of being drunk, to goad him into sharp replies, and then to attack. A boy that big, that strong looking, wouldn't be inclined to take too much from a smaller, older man. A quick right-leg kick, whatever throw suggested itself by the boy's reaction, and then some body work. A few broken ribs, perhaps a broken leg . . .

The boy raised his arm. A cab pulled up. The boy got inside and the cab drove off. Ted stood there a moment, then walked on, faster than before . . . walked as hard as he could.

He was still full of violence thirty blocks later when he turned the corner to the apartment house. He didn't see the car parked at the curb, nor the man getting out of it as he walked under the brick archway.

'Ted Barth?'

He whirled. A cop was coming toward him. Another sat in the prowl car at the curb. For a moment he thought he would fight them, or run. He had done so many things in the past nine months. And D'Andrea wanted to put him away for a 'cooling off' period. And he couldn't be put away – not now with so much at stake – with Susan at stake.

But they had guns and the day suddenly caught up with him and he was exhausted. 'Yes, I'm Ted Barth.'

The other cop was getting out of the car. The first cop said, 'Anything wrong, Mr Barth?' and came up close.

'No.'

'Lieutenant D'Andrea of Central Homicide sent us. He's been trying to get you for the past two, three hours. He said your line was busy.'

'Oh. Maybe I forgot to hang up.'

The cop was watching him closely. 'We tried your door. It was open and the light was on. We went in and the phone was on the floor.'

'It must have fallen.'

'D'Andrea was worried about you. Said to check you out.'

'Is that all?'

'No. He said to bring you in.'

'On what charge?'

'Charge? You been drinking, Mr Barth?'

Anger came. Anger at cops who entered his apartment uninvited – who spoke to him with sharp, wise-guy voices – who didn't catch the boy. 'What is it you want?'

'You remember who D'Andrea is, don't you? The detective in charge of your case. He wants you to identify something. You want to put it off till tomorrow 'cause you're not feeling good, okay. I'll just call in . . .'

'Identify something?'

The cop nodded.

The second cop came up and said, 'They brought in some stolen goods from a fence in Long Island City. Whole load of stuff on the sheet. Maybe something there that belongs to you.'

He asked if he could step into his apartment for a moment and they said sure. He went inside and closed the door and leaned against it, every pulse in his body pounding wildly. *'Maybe something there that belongs to you.'*

He washed his face with cold water, thought of a drink, then stood looking around the studio room. He was afraid to leave. He was afraid to go to D'Andrea and see what he had found. He was afraid it would be a false alarm.

He was just as afraid it would be a true lead.

If the search ended, he would have to face reality again. If the search ended, he would have to face himself again, without the streets, without the violence.

He lit a cigarette and shut the lights and went out. The first cop was waiting near the doorway. 'Cheer up, Mr Barth. This might be it.'

Ted nodded.

'You just gotta have faith.'

'Yes.'

'The lieutenant's worked harder on this case than on any I've ever seen. He's really pushing all the time.'

Ted went to the patrol car and got inside. He sat in the back alone, smoking a cigarette, watching the city flow by. When they stopped before the station house on the dingy West Side street, he could barely get out, his legs were so weak.

CHAPTER NINE

He was brought to a back room and told to take a seat. There were a dozen or more items on a table to his right, but he didn't look at them.

D'Andrea came in, wearing his glasses and his scholarly look. He smiled. 'Mr Barth. We're pretty sure we've got two items stolen from your apartment last November. Step over here, will you?'

Ted stood up and walked to the table. D'Andrea handed him a camera, a Nikon 35 mm. Ted saw the chip in the case – on the right side, when held ready for shooting. He examined the lens markings, the shutter speeds, and then fingered the chip. He nodded. 'Looks like it. Of course, if another Nikon were chipped in approximately the same spot . . .'

'How about this?' D'Andrea held out a ring.

There was no longer any room for doubt. The ruby had been his mother's, the one piece of real jewelry she had owned in all her life. It had stood surety for many loans, but before she died he reclaimed it for her, and she had given it to him. 'For your bride, someday. Tell her it came from your mother. Tell her it was given with love, with hope . . .'

He'd had the ring made for Myra – a yellow-gold snake in a double coil, head and tail forming the gem's setting. 'It's mine. Were they found together?'

'Same pawnshop. A known fence. And the same man pawned them.'

'You mean the same *boy* pawned them, don't you?'

'That's not important at the moment. You've made a positive identification. Now we can go ahead.'

'But it *was* a boy, wasn't it?'

D'Andrea shook his head. 'Elderly man. And just a few weeks ago.'

'How could it be? I saw that boy . . .'

'Mr Barth, you're not thinking clearly. The man who pawned these items could have been second or third along the line of people who purchased or handled them. Or he could have been acting for the boy, who held them until he thought they'd cooled off. Or he might even be a relative of the boy's, his father perhaps, who knowingly or not aided the boy in a felony.'

'What does he say?'

'We haven't got him. Not yet. He gave a phony address, as we expected. But there's a chance the man will return. He asked the fence how much he'd pay for a good transistor recorder. We've got the place staked out.'

'Where is it?'

'Long Island City.'

'Exactly where?'

D'Andrea took off his glasses, put them in a case and put the case in his breast pocket. 'You don't think I'd let you foul us up at this point, do you?'

Ted went back to the chair and sat down. It was almost three in the morning. He was dead. 'And if he doesn't come back, where are you?'

D'Andrea came across the room, the floorboards creaking beneath him. Ted realized what a big man he actually was. Almost Ted's height, but much shorter in appearance because of his thick, round body, a body that didn't seem to have an ounce of fat on it.

'Oh, we'll get him whether he comes back or not, Mr Barth. Count on that.'

'How can you be sure?'

'We have a sample of his handwriting. We have an excellent description and a witness who can identify him. We know what sort of car he was driving.' He smiled. 'We even know he belongs to an American Legion post right here in upper Manhattan. Our fence became quite anxious to help once he learned it was a double homicide. He remembered seeing the Legion membership card in the man's wallet when he opened it on the counter, and the post number.'

'Sounds good.'

'It is good. Let's hope he returns to the pawnshop. But even if he doesn't, we should have him soon.' He paused. 'Which brings me to something rather important. I want you to promise to drop your private search, at least for a month.'

'All right.'

D'Andrea seemed surprised. 'You mean that?'

'Yes.' Ted stood up. 'I was running out of belief in it

68

anyway. I need a rest. If you get the killer, it's over. If you don't, I can always start again. I lose nothing.' He couldn't help adding, 'I gain nothing.'

'What was that?'

Ted shook his head. 'The blues, Lieutenant. Haven't you ever had the blues?'

'In this business? Are you serious?' He stepped to the door. 'C'mon. I'll have someone drive you home.'

They walked down a grim corridor past rooms smelling of age and dust and fear. There was a great deal of fear in this building. Ted said, 'You'll let me know as soon as you find him, won't you?'

'I will, but you won't know the man.'

'I didn't mean him. I meant the boy, the killer.'

'Of course. You'll have to pick him out of a lineup.'

Ted nodded, then said, 'You won't mix him up with a lot of other boys the same age and height and coloring – the same type – will you?'

'Does the thought bother you?'

'It would kill me not to be sure.' He stopped near a door at the end of the hallway. 'I know him. I saw him and the night-light was on in the foyer. I'm sure I can pick him out of a group of people, different kinds of people. But if you stack the cards in his favor and I get confused . . .'

D'Andrea took his arm. 'Mr Barth, you're dreaming up plots – nightmares.'

'Well, what's the whole thing anyway but a nightmare?'

'But the police aren't part of it. We're going to get him. You can believe that now. We're going to get him, and we're not going to work against you in any way. He'll go into a lineup of cops and prisoners, not a group of boys picked to confuse you.'

'It's been nine months.' He felt sweat trickling down his face. 'I know I can recognize him, but it's been nine, almost ten months and I'm worried.'

'Take it easy,' D'Andrea muttered.

'I'll think of him. I'll think of him until his face stands out in my mind like it did that same night. He won't get away with it. I swear to you, he won't get away with it.'

'Mr Barth, Mr Barth,' D'Andrea said, voice pained. 'Sometimes I think that bastard killed more than . . .' He made a little palms-up gesture and opened the door to the desk room.

'When I get home, I'll go to bed. I'll sleep and I'll dream and I'll see him. I'll will myself to see him.' He was walking past the desk toward the street door. 'I'll remember his face just as if that night was last night.'

'I'll drive you home myself,' D'Andrea said.

'I'll see him from tonight until you catch him. He won't escape me. No, he won't escape me.'

The lieutenant caught him on the street. 'I said I'd drive you, Mr Barth.'

He allowed himself to be led to a car and placed inside. He didn't look at the streets as they drove. He looked into the past.

They stopped for a red light. The radio crackled with a riot call; Harlem, a bar brawl. Two women emerged from a doorway and crossed in front of the car. They were no longer young or very pretty, but their bodies were full and they displayed themselves in tight, bright dresses and languorous movements. One smiled invitingly, unaware that the unmarked car belonged to the police.

'Hookers,' D'Andrea muttered. 'What can they expect to get this time of night? Except maybe a knife up the ass.'

Ted watched them as D'Andrea pulled away. He wanted them. Just like that, he wanted their full bodies – any woman's full body. Those two girls from last night. He'd pay whatever they asked, if only he could find them.

D'Andrea said, 'You all right now, Mr Barth?'

'Fine.'

'Listen, I've got an idea. My wife and daughters are away at the shore. My place is roomy, comfortable. We even have air conditioning in the master bedroom. Why don't you come home with me? We'll have a few beers, play a little poker. You'll be doing me a favor.'

'No. I'm not sick. I just want to get to sleep.'

'I never said you were sick. I was thinking of something else. Something much more in my line of work.'

Ted looked at him.

'That kid might know we've picked up the stuff he stole. He might figure we're getting close. He will for sure once we nail the old man. Then what does he figure to do?'

70

'Leave the city?' Ted murmured.

'No. There are police all over. And he needs his friends, his pusher, maybe his girl. No, being the kind of nut he is, he'll probably try to get rid of the only eye-witness.'

Ted waited.

'He'll come looking for Ted Barth. And Ted Barth is easy to find, still living in the same building. Ted Barth is a sitting duck in that building. But I live halfway across the city. He'd never find you there. And if he did, I'd kill him.'

'And if he found me at my place *I'd* kill him.'

The lieutenant grunted.

'Besides, he couldn't get into my place. All the street-level windows in the house are barred, and that includes my two. There's no fire escape to use as he did that last time.' He smiled thinly. 'I think I'll stop locking my door.'

'That wouldn't be necessary. He could wait outside – catch you some night and go for you with his knife.'

'Let's hope so. Let's pray for it.'

The lieutenant said nothing more until they reached the house; then he asked if he could come in for a drink.

'On duty?'

'I've always been a lousy cop that way.'

They had a bourbon and water together. The lieutenant said, 'Think I'll have one more. Go ahead and get ready for bed. I'll smoke another butt . . .'

'And then you'll tuck me in, sing a lullaby and fly out the window with Peter Pan and Wendy.'

The lieutenant laughed and went to the door. 'I guess that's the gist of it. Try to stay alive until that lineup, Mr Barth. And then, until the trial. After that . . .' He looked at Ted, his laughter gone.

'After that I'll start to live again.'

'Sure,' the lieutenant said. He seemed about to say something more, then waved his hand and left.

Ted walked the streets, looking not for the boy, but for a woman. He found no woman. He returned to his apartment when the night sky was bleached by approaching sunrise. He undressed and opened the sleeper couch and lay down.

He slept, but bloody dreams tore at him and he awakened. He lay drenched in morning sunlight and sweat – and he remembered.

71

A Wednesday night in November. He had worked late. He had been working late the last three nights. It was nine thirty when he entered the apartment. Myra said she hoped he was feeling all right. He had been fighting a cold. The late hours hadn't helped. And the heavy smoking. He had a sore throat – a flushed, feverish feeling.

She served him dinner. He wasn't very hungry. She pressed him to eat, and he snapped at her – something about her being his wife, not his Momma. She answered with tears, and they each dredged up a few bad memories to throw at the other. But later, after looking in on Debbie, he made up with Myra, pleading exhaustion and his cold, and went to sleep in the den that doubled as a guestroom.

He didn't know how long he slept, but there was a sound and he awoke. He heard footsteps and sat up in bed. A shape entered the doorway, coming from the direction of the master bedroom and Debbie's room. It was going toward the kitchen and the living room. He began to say Myra's name, but the figure paused and he saw it wasn't Myra, wasn't Debbie, wasn't anyone who belonged in this apartment.

It was a boy, and he was illuminated by the nightlight a few feet back up the foyer. A boy – and Ted saw the face, saw the hair, saw the cloth jacket and tight, black pants. Saw the wild, hard, challenging look.

And then the boy ran. And Ted got up . . .

He stopped it there, before the true horror could engulf him. He had remembered all that was necessary: the boy – exactly what the boy looked like.

He lay down again and closed his eyes again and held to the image in his mind.

CHAPTER TEN

He slept until three P.M., waking with sunlight lying hot across his chest and stomach. He woke with the boy's face still clear in his mind. He saw the thin lower lip, the heavily curved upper lip, the thick, brown hair piled high in front, the short, sharp nose, the lean cheeks, the narrow eyes that could have been blue, could have been gray, the totality of hardness in face and body. He got up ... went to the dresser ... found the envelope and took out the sheet of paper. He read the description he had written down two days after the murders – the description he had given D'Andrea. It matched the picture in his mind. He put away the envelope. He didn't need it. He would recognize that boy anywhere.

He showered and dressed and had eggs and coffee; then he called Susan at Drizer Chemical. 'Are we on for Saturday night?'

'I'm afraid not, Ted'.

Arthur.

'But Sunday would be fine. Think we could get a car and drive out to the shore?'

'Yes.'

'We can make it early. As early as nine thirty or ten if you like. We can have the whole day – swimming at Jones Beach. I'll pack a basket of goodies. All right?'

She was gentling him: a nurse soothing a patient; a mother comforting a disappointed child. But he was tired of that. He wanted something else from her – something more.

'All right, Ted?'

'Yes.'

'Well ... see you Sunday.' Her voice questioned him, worried by his silences.

'Yes Sunday. I'll rent a convertible.'

'That'll be fun. I haven't ridden in a convertible since I moved to the city and Dad sold my little Triumph. Here it's buses or subways or cabs.'

'Not really?'

She laughed, thinking he was joking, and in a way he was.

And in a way he wasn't joking; he was raging. They said goodbye.

It was four thirty. He was sorry he hadn't thought to ask her to dinner tonight. Should he call her back?

Instinct told him to concentrate on Sunday. But longing made him pick up the phone and dial again and speak to her again. 'I was just thinking. Here I am eating alone tonight, and there you are, eating alone tonight . . .'

'Hank and I are eating in Tarrytown tonight with the family.'

'Oh.' He knew he should chuckle and say better-luck-next-time and hang up. He said, 'Tomorrow night?'

'I'm staying home and washing my hair and catching up on some reading. *Goodbye*, Ted.'

'*Goodbye*, Susan,' he said, imitating her sharpness, hoping to draw a laugh.

He drew a click and a dead line.

He checked the mail. Two ads and a letter for Myra. He had gotten mail for her before, but not for some months now. He looked at the return address. Los Angeles. He considered destroying it unread. He had considered that before but had never been able to do it.

He opened it. It was from a girl named Nancy Pinto. She had gone to Vassar with Myra. 'I've just been thinking of you and wondering what's happened in the three years since we last saw each other. (By the way, have you read *The Group*?) Hope you still live at the same address. How are Debbie and your husband? (Forgive me, I can't remember his name. He was never home the afternoons we met.) George and I are doing nicely. The weather here is what I always dreamed of. Spring all year long . . .' He scanned descriptions of children and houses and movie stars, then tore the letter up and threw it in the waste basket. That life was finished – in the wastebasket.

Spring all year long. He and Susan could move to Los Angeles. No reason to stay in New York. Soon as they caught the boy, he could ask her . . .

He was afraid to think of her now, after the coldness she had shown.

Arthur. Arthur taking her out this Saturday. Arthur kissing her in the shadows.

74

He could go to Los Angeles, with or without Susan. Spring all year long. New people. No more Laura and Betsy and memories and guilt.

He sat down and leaned back and closed his eyes. He dreamed of a new life, a normal life. He would start preparing for it today.

He would go to movies again. He hadn't seen a movie in nine months, or a play, a concert, an opera – all things he had once enjoyed.

He would read more – not just newspapers, but books. He had barely opened a book in nine months, and he had loved novels, especially historicals.

He would start attending judo class regularly.

He would begin again to enjoy himself, to participate in life. He would train himself for enjoyment, for participation.

The phone rang. It was Laura. She said they were leaving for their vacation Saturday morning. They wanted him over Friday night, as usual, for dinner.

He said, 'You'll need that last night for packing, getting the kids to bed ...'

'Nonsense. You're coming and that's all. Wallace will pick you up about five thirty.'

He said, 'No', very quietly.

'What?'

'No. I'm sorry. It's too much ... Betsy and the family feeling and all. I won't come. Not for a while, anyway.'

When she tried to argue the point, he said he was just leaving for a job interview. When she tried to ask questions about the job, he said goodbye and hung up. He stood near the phone, smiling tightly. He had finally done it. At last the painful knot was cut. Let her think whatever she wanted to now. Let her think he was a promiscuous bastard who had married Myra for her money. Let her. He wouldn't see her anymore, ever again, and he didn't care if she ...

And then he realized what he had thought and remembered what he had never really forgotten. Laura – dancing with him that night twelve, thirteen years ago, shortly before he and Myra were married. He was holding her tight against him, letting his manhood rise, letting her feel it, forcing her to stay close against him, pressing his lips to her ear, her neck, watching as Wallace and Myra danced at the other

75

side of the hotel ballroom, laughing as Laura muttered, 'Ted, for the love of heaven!'

The music stopped but he held onto her, murmuring that it would start again in a moment and that he was enjoying her and that she was really a lovely girl a desirable girl, and wasn't it too bad they were going to be related. She tore loose and hurried across the floor. The music started and Wallace and Myra continued dancing and he and Laura sat alone at the table. He laughed at her tight, closed face. He said, 'Now be forgiving to your future brother-in-law. He had one martini too many.'

That was when she looked at him. That was when she said, 'I know you, Ted Barth,' her voice cold as only Laura could make her voice cold.

He tried to laugh away the chill. He said, 'Sure you do. I'm a man. Like a dozen men you must've dated.'

'No, not like a dozen men I dated.' Cold, cold voice. Sharp, cold eyes. 'I know you. I know your type. Like one man I dated.'

He said, 'Aha, a lost love,' and watched the dancing couples.'

'You care nothing for Myra,' she said.

He had to turn then – had to protest. 'That's not very bright, is it, since I'm marrying her in four weeks.'

She never looked away. It was he who looked away. She looked at him, into him, and he suddenly feared and hated her. Why the hell had he bothered with the skinny little bitch? 'What an idiotic thing to say. A man has a drink or two and feels playful . . .'

'Other times you didn't have a drink or two and you still felt playful. With me. With Terry, Sam's girl. With my cousin Phyl. With anyone and everyone who . . .'

'Now don't tell me I made passes at *you* before?'

'Yes. Not like this, not as obvious, but you asked, in one way or another, for my encouragement. If it had been given, you'd have gone further. My cousin Phyl's a talker. You made a mistake there. She felt guilty after the second time and stopped seeing you and then just had to get it off her chest – to me.'

His face grew hot. 'She's a liar. A dreamer. I patted her rump.'

'Terry's not a talker, but I see the way she looks at you. Or *looked* at you, before you said you didn't like Sam and cut them out of our dates. She likes you too much, doesn't she, Ted? You won't risk losing Myra.'

That's when he made his mistake. Not thinking, he snapped, 'And why should I worry about losing Myra if I care nothing for her?'

The music ended as she smiled. Lousy, withered, hateful smile! 'When did you ever know a girl with over a hundred thousand dollars in her own name?'

He put as much shock and contempt into his expression as he could. She didn't back down a bit. Myra and Wallace were coming toward the table. 'Tell her that, why don't you?' he said, and rose to greet his fiancée.

'I would if I thought there was any chance she'd believe me. But she's in love. She doesn't see anything she doesn't want to see. And it takes a particular kind of eye to see what a sharp, promiscuous bastard you are.'

Wallace and Myra were there. He was particularly attentive to Myra the rest of the evening. But every so often he caught Laura's eye, and it was a knowing, cynical eye, and he couldn't laugh off what she had said.

They had one more chance to speak alone – on the street, walking down Fifth Avenue, when Wallace and Myra stepped over to a shop window and left them near the curb. He said, 'Could it be that you hate me for marrying into what you consider *your* inheritance – the money Wallace feels should have been his?'

'No, it couldn't be.' She was unshakable, with her damned eyes cutting into him.

'Then perhaps you doubt your own feelings?'

The eyes wavered for just an instant, and he pressed on with a vengeance.

'Perhaps Wallace is not quite your dream of young love. Perhaps you're settling for what you can get and you want something else – something, could it be, like the sharp, promiscuous bastard ...'

'Maybe.'

He smiled.

'Scratch any girl about to get married and you'll find uncertainty, last-minute dreams of other men. But it doesn't

77

change what I know, what I sense about *you*. The marriage won't last.'

'Want to bet?'

She turned away then, murmuring, 'Well, I hope I'm wrong. And if I am ... maybe I also had one drink too many – with my one drink.'

Her moment of doubt hadn't helped. He had suffered over that evening for quite a while, even after the wedding; then a quarrel between Myra and Wallace made it easy to keep their meetings at a minimum. Even after the births of Debbie and Betsy, when they had begun seeing each other – even then he had remembered and resented Laura. Even after his success at Drizer was assured, even after she had obviously forgotten that evening and had grown to like him – even then he had been unable to forgive her. Because, he had reasoned, every man had desires, had weaknesses and areas of guilt, and with someone like Laura around he couldn't forget them, couldn't relax with his family, couldn't accept himself for what he was.

But resentment had finally died. For the past four or five years he had accepted Laura as his sister-in-law and friend. They saw each other several times a month. He had forgotten that evening as completely as she had. Until the murders ... and even then he hadn't known exactly what was bothering him with Laura. Until this week. Until now. Until that memory had been pulled from the shadows and fully exposed.

Exposed for the foolishness it was.

He decided to go to a movie. And later to attend the weekly meeting of his judo class.

He walked to a theater between Third and Lex that was showing a highly rated Italian comedy. As he turned to the glass ticket booth, he saw the boy. The boy who had been walking behind him. The boy who now hurried past, ducking his head.

The aging blond said, 'How many, sir?'

He stared after the boy, heart hammering.

'Sir?'

He hesitated, hand on his wallet, and then started after the boy. So many had been close. But this one had the right hair: the right color and piled high. And the face, the

78

glimpse he'd had of it, had also been right. The clothes were different – tan slacks and a green, short-sleeved shirt – but it was summer now.

The boy turned the corner onto Lexington Avenue. Ted wanted to run but remembered his decision to prepare for a new life – a normal life. Chasing after every passing kid was the old way – the sick way.

But what if this was the right one? He hadn't been looking for the boy. The boy had been *behind* him, perhaps following . . .

He began to run. A woman gasped as he brushed past her. He turned the corner. He didn't see the boy for a moment, and then he did. He was just getting on a bus near the opposite corner. He must have run for it.

Ted sprinted, then stopped as the bus moved away. He looked around for a cab, then looked after the bus, then stopped looking for a cab. He told himself it was just another kid – another brown-haired, hard-faced kid. The city was full of them.

He turned back toward the theater. It was hot and sweat trickled down his face. His heart still hammered. Just another kid, he told himself. Just another kid.

His heart wouldn't slow down and the sweat wouldn't stop trickling, not even after half an hour in the dark, cool theater. Had he missed that one-in-a-million chance?

But one in a million was hardly believable odds.

If it was the right boy, he hadn't been walking behind Ted by chance. He had been following him, as D'Andrea had said he might, waiting to use his knife on the only person who could place him in the apartment the night of the murders.

But in broad daylight? At four thirty of a bright August afternoon?

He made himself think it through and began to grow calm. It probably wasn't the boy. Those were the odds. But if it was, he hadn't accomplished what he had set out to do. He hadn't eliminated the one eyewitness. Therefore, he would have to follow Ted again – at night now that he had cased his victim. At night for the payoff.

Ted would have to give him plenty of opportunity.

CHAPTER ELEVEN

The *dojo* for advanced judo was the main gym of the big 47th Street Gym. Class met Thursday evenings, 8:30 to 10:00. Ted walked downtown along First Avenue, carrying an airline bag containing his *gi* – the heavy cotton jacket and light, knee-length cotton trousers that a *judoka* wears during combat. Before the murders this walk had been a preparatory period in which he had reviewed the previous week's lessons and planned his night's work – perhaps getting Lloyd Berdon, the strong, colored first *dan* black belter as his partner and concentrating on *shime waza*, the art of strangulation, or Adrian Rosenstein who was so quick at *ogoshi*, *osoto gari* and other throws that he was excellent competition despite his lowly fourth *kyu* rating.

Not this night. This night he thought only of who might be behind him. This night he stopped for a traffic light and glanced over his shoulder and wondered if there was someone standing in that doorway fifty feet away.

He turned down 47th Street and reached the gym and paused before the doors, as if waiting for someone. He looked around. He saw no one, though back on the avenue, on the far side of the street, people walked – and one was a swaggering boy and he could be the one.

He entered the building and walked past the information desk to the staircase and up to the second floor. He handed his membership card and a dime to the old man at the counter and said, 'judo'. He took the locker key and towel and walked around the corner to the right and down a short corridor. Even before he reached the locker room, the oniony smell of stale sweat greeted him. A moment later he had to stop short as a heavily muscled youth came nude and dripping from the shower room. He was of medium height, his hair brown, his face hard.

Ted stared after him. Would he know the boy nude and dripping wet in a locker room? Would a murderous narcotics addict work out in a gym?

The youth stopped at a locker, opened it and turned. Ted

decided the face was all wrong, the body too wide. He went down the center aisle to his locker, undressed and got into his *gi*. He sat on his stool, facing the open locker, smoking away the five minutes that remained until class began. Behind him two men entered and began to talk and laugh. Then their voices dropped and all he heard were murmurs. When he left for the main gym, they were standing at adjoining lockers, facing each other nude. They moved farther apart as he passed, but he read their excitement. One of them greeted him with a quick nod. He was a burly man in his mid-forties, an extremely tough member of the judo class, very close to his black belt. Ted had faced him several times in the *randori* – the combat period – and had emerged victor only once. So much for the supposed feminine weakness of homosexuals. Any self-styled tough who tried to ruffle *that* gay one's feathers would be lucky to come away alive.

The *dojo* was all set up. Mats were spread under the far basket of what was normally a basketball court; a tarpaulin covered them, making a single padded floor 35 feet by 35 feet, considerably over the official 30 by 30 contest area but a convenience because of the size of certain classes. The advanced class, however, never numbered over six students. Tonight there were only Ted, Lloyd Berdon, the burly homosexual Ted knew as Calora, and the *shihan*, their instructor, Tom Honda. Honda was a slender Japanese-American, a *yudansha* second grade who had taken both grades at the *Kodokwan*, the university of judo in Tokyo. He came across the mat and onto the wood floor, bare feet slapping softly, to greet Ted. 'Good to see you,' he said. 'Going to work out a little?'

Ted slipped off his thonged shoes and moved his right shoulder experimentally. It was still slightly stiff from the cop's nightstick. 'I hope to start attending class regularly.'

'Good,' Honda said. 'You can see how we've shrunk. Rosenstein tore a muscle in his leg and he'll be out awhile. Pegget took a job in the Midwest and moved away. Without you, we were cut in half.'

On the mat, Ted and the other three students lined up at one end; Honda faced them from the other end, under the basket. The students went to their knees and bowed until

81

their heads touched the mat. The *shihan* bowed from the waist, accepting their homage. Then he announced a loosening-up period. They did fifty Japanese sit-ups, hands crossed on chest, knees up at about a forty-five-degree angle. Ted found his stomach was still in good shape, and completed the fifty without difficulty. Then fifteen push-ups, fifteen between-the-legs mat touches, fifteen side-to-side swivels and fifteen squats.

'Falls,' Honda announced, and collapsed backward, slapping his arms on the mat to stop his movement. They did the backward fall fifteen times. Ted began to breathe heavily and perspire lightly.

The side falls were next, the right arm breaking the fall to the right side, the left arm to the left side. These were followed by the forward breakfall.

A forward roll completed the loosening-up period, each student running across the mat catercorner, rolling over on his curved right arm, coming erect and trotting off the mat. Honda patted Ted on the back. 'You're nice and loose,' he murmured. 'Looks like you been working out.'

Ted smiled slightly. Honda would be surprised at how much 'working out' was forced on anyone who walked the city's streets at night. He returned to the mat, paired with Lloyd Berdon, and Honda called for them to practice the resisting hip throw. Berdon was a tall, lean, long-muscled Negro whose specialty was aggressive *katame-no-kata*, or groundwork. He was also expert, partly because of his height, in resisting certain throws.

Taking turns, they neatly frustrated each other's attacks. Ted deliberately avoided feinting or bluffing the first five times to establish an expectation of head-on attempt in Berdon's mind. Then, after foiling Berdon's third double feint, he grasped his opponent's *gi*, started to move in low, hesitated, and continued with all the speed he could muster. He turned, his buttocks hitting Berdon's right thigh, screamed the *keeyi* and jerked forward. Berdon went over and slammed the mat, landing well but looking up at Ted with quick anger. Ted reached down to help him. Berdon rolled away and rose on his own. Honda came over. 'Unfair advantage, Ted.'

'How?'

'The *keeyi.*'

'Good God!' He didn't see how he could have forgotten that Honda had put a restriction on the shrill scream that shocked an opponent, froze him for a moment and threw him off balance. They weren't supposed to use it, just as they weren't supposed to use the sudden ejaculation of spittle into an opponent's face. Just as they weren't supposed to use certain leg, wrist and finger locks. Just as they weren't supposed to use so many effective blows.

He turned to Berdon and said he was sorry. Berdon's face cleared. He shrugged and said, 'Let's go.'

Ted fully intended to relax and take a fall to even the score with Berdon. But he couldn't. He resisted all the way. As soon as Berdon's hands closed on his *gi* and he moved to the attack, Ted began to fight. It was all he could do to remain on the defensive and not strike back before his turn.

Honda called a halt and had Berdon work out with him, using *butsukari,* the system of aborting throws so that no one actually fell. Ted watched, trying to study the *shihan's* technique, but found he was impatient, irritated with the lack of action, and with the openings he saw for quick demolition of an opponent – openings ignored in the ritual of judo sportsmanship.

Honda then announced the *randori.* He called on Ted and Calora for *katame-no-kata.* Ted had fought the burly man in throws, but never in groundwork. They knelt, right leg down, left leg up, left hand on left knee, facing each other at a distance of about three feet. Honda called '*Hajime!*' and they went at each other. Within seconds, Ted knew that here was where his lack of consistent class attendance and weekly workouts would cost him. Calora was an inch or two under Ted's five eleven, but he must have weighed ten pounds more than Ted's 170. And most of that weight was in the upper portion of his body, a thick and powerful torso set on relatively short, thin legs.

After the initial scrabbling for position, Ted found himself in *uke's* posture, bottom man in a *kesa gatame,* pinned flat on his back with Calora's damp head under his chin. He managed to break out with an elbow in Calora's neck, but was immediately back as bottom man in *kuzure wami shiho.* This was a hold in which the top man crouched with his

83

knees behind the bottom man's head and his head in the bottom man's lower abdomen, keeping him pinned with the weight of his body and his hands clasped under the bottom man's back. It was close to the sexual position called 69, and Ted remembered Calora's excitement in the locker room and was revolted. He fought with heaving, bucking motions, but Calora's weight and strength were too much. He resolved to wait out the thirty seconds which would automatically give Calora an *ippon*, or full victory, and thus end the hold.

But Calora shifted position, sliding farther down along Ted's body, and revulsion grew and panic grew and the redness came. He could hear Honda's voice instructing at the other end of the mat, and was afraid that the *shihan* would be slow in calling an *ippon*. And then he felt Calora move once again. The man's lower body pressed his face and he thought he felt a change in that body and he surged upward and reached back desperately and found Calora's foot. He grasped a toe and twisted, which was enough to cause *hansoku-make*, loss by foul. Calora cried out and raised himself and Ted brought up his knees and hands and lunged out in stiff-fingered karate attack and Calora screamed and pounded down with both fists at Ted's belly. But Ted had already twisted onto his side, rolling to the right, and was freed and came bounding up. Calora was on one knee, grimacing, hands to his left side. Ted kicked him under the chin. Calora's head snapped back and he fell and lay still. Ted stepped toward him, the redness complete now, ready to kick the man's brains out.

Someone spun him around. He grasped a *gi* and ducked to butt. His movement was stopped by a terrible blow to the stomach. He fell backward, but was able to tuck in his chin and give himself impetus to go completely over and come to his feet. As he did, he threw himself to the left and caught the foot that lashed at his chest. He turned his back on his opponent and held to the foot and swung around to the left and kept swinging until he knew his opponent couldn't possibly hop with the movement and was falling. Then he let go and completed the turn and leaped high in the air to come down on where his opponent should have been. His opponent, however, was rolling frantically across the mat. Ted leaped after him to kick him before he had a chance to rise.

Someone caught his belt from behind. He gave his *keeyi* and swung about. It was the colored *judoka*, Berdon, shouting, 'That's the *shihan*, Ted! That's the *shihan*!'

He kicked at Berdon's stomach, missed, staggered. At the same time he was chopped on the back of the neck and went numb and found himself lying on the mat. The man sitting on his back applied an agonizing, right wrist lock. He was held. The redness began to lift. Honda's voice said, 'I'm going to let go now. I want you to get up and walk to the locker room. Don't turn. Don't even look back. I'll be watching. I'll use everything on you if you stop. I want you to leave. I don't want you to come back.'

Ted said, 'All right. But he, Calora . . .'

'I don't want to hear. You broke every rule. You're dangerous. If it wasn't for your trouble, I'd call the police.'

His wrist was released. The weight left his back. He got to his feet, facing Honda. Behind the *shihan*, Berdon stood over Calora, who was sitting up, blood trickling from his mouth. Honda said, 'Turn. Walk.'

Ted turned and walked. Not that he was afraid of Honda. On the street, with shoes and clothing and no holds barred, he felt he could take the slender Japanese. But there was no longer any sense to it. He was drained and empty. Six years of judo was finished. He could no longer hold to the rules and regulations. He admitted it to himself. He had used too much *jujitsu* on the streets – too much free-for-all combat technique. And the redness came too swiftly, too often.

He showered and packed his *gi* and came out onto 47th Street. He walked back to First Avenue and turned uptown. It wasn't quite ten and he had slept late, but he was tired. His shoulder hurt. His neck hurt. His right wrist hurt. He wanted a sandwich, a few drinks and bed.

He glanced around a few times, but didn't see anyone like the boy and didn't really expect to. His excitement at the movie now seemed like all the other excitements of the past nine months. Imagination. A sickness of the mind.

He wondered if Susan was really in Tarrytown, wondered whether he should go to her 82nd Street apartment and ring the bell to see for himself. If she answered, he could always say he had just been passing by.

But he didn't want to catch her in a lie. He didn't want to catch her with Arthur. He'd had enough hate and violence for one day. His body cried for rest; his mind for peace.

He stopped at a delicatessen and bought a sandwich and potato salad and two bottles of German beer. He had the makings in his refrigerator, but wanted to relax thoroughly – not do a thing but eat and drink and sleep.

He came to the brick archway and there was no police car and no one to stop him from his evening of rest and peace. He smiled a little, grateful for small favors, went inside, locked the door and threw the light switch. Then he saw the envelope on the floor, where someone had shoved it under the door.

He put his package on the coffee table and went back to the door and picked up the envelope; it was white and business size and blank. He opened it and took out a sheet of white paper. As soon as he unfolded it, his evening of rest and peace was over.

The letters had been cut out of a newspaper. They varied in size from headline type to subhead to small print, and were pasted on the sheet to form words – five lines of words.

'Barth. I won't let you do it to me. Don't try. I kill you first. I swear I know you. I see you. I get you. Stop it now.'

He heard a harsh sound and looked up and realized it was his own breath. He dropped the letter to prevent himself from ripping it, tearing it, destroying it. But his rage, his fury, continued to mount.

'He won't let me do it to him,' he whispered.

He raised his foot to stamp on the obscenity, but didn't. D'Andrea would get that letter. D'Andrea would use it as yet another nail in the boy's coffin. They must be getting close to him now, or else he wouldn't have sent the letter. They must be making him sweat.

He picked up the letter. 'I know you,' he read. 'I see you.'

The boy at the movie! The boy following him!

He turned to the door. He wanted to step outside and look around. But he didn't. The boy wouldn't be standing there. He was smarter than that.

He opened the Yale lock and pressed down the button that would keep it open. He unhooked the chain lock; it would remain off tonight and every night until the boy was

86

finished. He went to the phone and dialed Central Homicide and asked for D'Andrea. A strange voice answered D'Andrea's extension. 'The lieutenant's out right now. Can I help you?'

'Please tell him to call Ted Barth.'

'I'll do that, Mr Barth. He's out on a pickup connected with your case. Better stay close to your phone.'

Ted wanted to ask questions, but the line clicked so he sat down and waited. After a while he remembered his sandwich. He ate it and the potato salad. He drank both beers even though they weren't very cold. He sat near the phone and smoked.

He must have dozed off, because he came to with a start. The phone was ringing. He picked it up and said, 'Yes?'

There was no answer.

'This is Ted Barth,' he said. 'Hello.'

'I won't let you do it,' the fogged, disguised, whispering voice said. 'I warn you, I won't.'

He stood up. The line went dead. He held the phone awhile, then put it back in the cradle and stood waiting for it to ring. It rang. He raised it, trying to control his breathing. D'Andrea's voice said, 'Hello? Hello, Mr Barth?'

He said yes and slumped into his chair. His hands were wet. He took out his handkerchief and wiped them, propping the phone between ear and shoulder. The lieutenant said, 'I got a message you called. Anything wrong?'

He hesitated. That phone call changed things. That phone call brought the boy very close. If he told D'Andrea about the call and the letter, he would get a police guard whether he wanted one or not. And he didn't want one. He wanted the boy.

'Nothing's wrong. I was wondering if you'd made any progress.'

'We have.' Satisfaction was evident in the lieutenant's voice. 'Our stakeout in Long Island City paid off. We got the old man who pawned the camera and the ring. He had your tape recorder. He claims they were left in the basement of the tenement where he's the janitor. He says he kept the money himself, didn't know the items were stolen, doesn't know any boy who fits the description of the killer.'

'Do you believe him?'

'D'Andrea laughed.

'But it could be the truth. The boy might have decided to dump the stolen items after realizing what he'd done. He might have decided they could be traced to him.'

'Not a boy like that. Not a boy who killed for a fix or two. We'll sweat the old man tonight. We'll make him tell his story over and over. We'll catch him in little lies. Then he'll lead us to the boy. Tonight, tomorrow, maybe the day after – but he'll lead us to the boy.'

'Can I come down?'

'What for? You won't know him.'

'Let him see me. Let him see what's left of a family. Let him know he's protecting someone who took everything from me.'

'All right. Want me to send a patrol car?'

'I'll catch a cab.'

He hung up and went to the door. He picked up the envelope and the letter from the floor, carried them to the dresser and hid them under a pile of linen. He put out the lights and left the apartment. Outside he checked to make sure the door was open. He hoped the boy would be waiting for him when he returned. He prayed for it.

CHAPTER TWELVE

At Central Homicide he was taken from the desk to the same room in back where he had identified the camera and the ring. D'Andrea entered a moment later. 'Our janitor is demanding his rights. A call and a lawyer and everything else. But we've found his record. He's been up for narcotics peddling, narcotics addiction, armed robbery, indecent exposure and statutory rape. A good, solid citizen. The D.A. won't worry about his rights for a day or two, and I want to keep him alone and afraid.'

'That's illegal,' Ted said.

'That's right. Want to enter a complaint?'

Ted smiled faintly. The lieutenant bent to a cardboard carton under the table and took out a small transistor recorder. Ted walked over and looked at it. 'Take it,' D'Andrea said. Ted took it. He turned it over and nodded. 'It's the same type and model. It's mine, far as I know.'

'Matches the serial number you gave us. It's yours.'

'It had a case.'

'We've got it. There's a partially used tape on the machine.'

Ted remembered. He put the recorder on the table.

'You can have it, along with the camera and the ring when it's served its purpose as evidence.'

Ted touched the mounted spool. 'Can I play it now?'

D'Andrea walked to the door. 'You don't have to plug it in. The battery's still good.'

Ted was alone. He threw the 'Play' lever and heard his own voice.

'. . . just the way I'm speaking. Right into the little mike.'

'Here?' Debbie's voice said.

'That's right. Now recite it the way you did in school.'

'You'll hear yourself, honey,' Myra's voice said in the background. 'In a few minutes you'll hear yourself speaking.'

Ted turned and walked away and stopped only when he reached the wall.

'Okay,' his voice said. 'Start.'

'Between the dark and the daylight
When the night is beginning to lower
Comes a pause in the day's occupation . . .'

The thin voice erupted in giggles.

'Come on now,' he heard himself say. 'Once through – the way you did it in school.'

'Between the dark and the daylight.'

He turned and went to the recorder.

'When the night . . .'

He switched it off.

'Between the dark and the daylight,' the child's voice ran on in his head. *'Between the dark and the daylight.'*

'That is known as the Children's Hour,' he whispered, exorcizing the voice.

But it wasn't until D'Andrea came in that the voice stopped.

They went up the grim hall away from the door leading to the street. There were stairs at the end and they went down to a basement area. It was even grimmer here: a wide corridor with a blank wall on the left and three cages on the right. The light was harsh and glaring from bare bulbs in metal-reflector fixtures covered by wire mesh.

D'Andrea stopped in front of the first cage. It was occupied by a thin man with wispy, gray hair sitting on the edge of a metal cot. He looked up, then stood up; and Ted saw he was quite old – at least seventy. He had a lined, narrow face and a large bulbous nose. He wore a blue suit and a white shirt without a tie. The suit was rumpled and much too big for him. He said, 'This one of them free lawyers?' His voice was unexpectedly strong.

'This is the man who owns the recorder and other things you pawned – the man whose wife and child were killed.'

The old man looked at Ted and then quickly away. 'That's nothing to do with me,' he said, but his voice lost some of its strength. 'I just found 'em. When you gonna let me make my call?'

'You're going to die in prison,' D'Andrea said. 'You know that, don't you, Abel?'

90

'Why won't you let me call my wife? I'm allowed . . .'

'Tell me,' Ted whispered, moving up against the bars, gripping them. 'Who gave you those things? Tell me.'

The old man backed up and bumped into the edge of the cot. He moved away from the cot to the far wall. 'I told the police. No one *gave* them to me – they was left in the basement.'

'Tell me,' Ted whispered. 'I have a right to know. You can see that, can't you?'

The old man spread his hands.

'It's terrible if you know and won't tell.'

'Look,' the old man said to D'Andrea, his voice cracking. 'You got no right to let him . . . I got rights too. Take him away. I won't talk to him. Take him away.' He turned his back.

Ted stepped away from the bars. 'If he knows, then he's as bad as the boy. He's guilty too. He's a murderer too.'

The old man turned and shouted, 'He said it was a lie. He swore . . .' He stopped, eyes fixed on D'Andrea.

The lieutenant smiled and nodded. 'Who swore, Abel?'

'I mean . . .'

'What do you mean, Abel?'

'I'm an old man,' Abel muttered. 'I get mixed up.'

'Your record certainly backs *that* statement.'

'I've been clean for years and years,' the old man muttered.

'Who said it was a lie, Abel?'

The old man moved toward the cot.

'We've got men questioning your tenants right now, Abel. Someone saw you with that boy. Is he a relative?'

Abel shook his head. 'I'm an old man. I'm sick. I got diabetes.'

'We'll get you a doctor. Tell me, Abel. Who swore?'

The old man lowered himself to the cot and lay down, face to the wall.

'Okay. Rest awhile, Abel. I'll be back. Then we'll go upstairs and have some coffee and you'll tell me who swore it was a lie. Receiving stolen goods is a small rap, Abel. Accessory to Murder One is something else again.'

The old man shook his head. 'I got diabetes,' he muttered. 'I got bone sickness.'

D'Andrea took Ted's arm and led him through the door. 'You were right,' he said. 'His seeing you was helpful. Go on home now.'

Ted rode home with two policemen. He accepted the cigarette one offered him and sat quietly in the rear. He didn't look out at the city. That was finished. Soon the boy would come to him.

In front of the apartment he thanked the officers and waited until they were gone. Then he went to the brick archway and put his hand on the door. He opened it and gave it a push and crouched. The moment it touched the wall he threw himself inside. He landed on his hands and knees and came upright and twisted around. He held his breath and listened.

The refrigerator hummed. A man and a woman came by the open door and the woman glanced inside. A toilet flushed upstairs.

He went into the studio room and turned slowly, body coiled, hands shoulder-high and ready for chopping. He stopped and said, 'Let's get it over with. I'm waiting.' But he knew he was alone. He went to the door and closed it and put on the light.

He showered. He had a bourbon. He dressed in fresh slacks and a polo shirt. He had another bourbon and smoked a cigarette. He was terribly tired. The beginning of this day seemed to stretch back to another lifetime, another century. And yet, it was still a few minutes shy of midnight when he left the apartment.

He walked the streets. He cut down dark side streets, inviting the boy to make his play. He moved gradually uptown, heading for Susan's place without realizing it until he was a block away. Then he walked by and saw that the shade was up and that it was dark inside. She was either asleep or had stayed at her parents' home for the night. (*Or was somewhere with Arthur.* But he wouldn't think of that. Saturday, when he knew for sure, he would think of it and do something to change it.)

He started back downtown. His legs ached. His body sagged with fatigue. He wondered whether he could handle the boy if he attacked now. And still thinking that, he turned west, toward the bad streets. He would keep going until his legs were about to fold. Then he would find a cab and ride home.

It was one of those dying streets near Tenth Avenue. Half the houses were boarded up, marked for the wrecker's iron ball. The other half were only partly occupied – by the helpless aged and the hopeless dregs. He heard a girl's voice. She said one word, a four-letter obscenity, but she said it sweetly, with promise. He stopped. She was standing in the doorway of an otherwise boarded-up tenement.

He said, 'Come down where I can see you.'

She said, 'Baby, you come up where I can touch you.'

He mounted three stone steps. She came a little farther out of the doorway. 'Five dollars, baby.'

She was tall and plump – a childish plumpness. She was colored, quite dark, with a round, pretty face untouched by makeup. She wore a dark skirt, a white blouse and shiny, black, high-heeled shoes. She looked at least fourteen.

'I could get five years for my five dollars worth,' he said. 'You're an infant.'

She came out of the doorway and moved into him. She didn't waste time, but used her hands to get to the root of the matter. He began to breathe hard, but didn't touch her.

'You'd like an infant like me, wouldn't you, daddy?' She put her lips up and waited. He lowered his head. Their lips touched. She bit him lightly and spoke into his mouth.

'I'm thirteen. You ever have an infant thirteen years old? That's worth more than five dollars, ain't it, daddy?'

He didn't answer.

'C'mon, daddy, this infant just wet her pants for you.' She withdrew her hands. 'C'mon inside.'

'In there? That's a dead house.'

'I got a live little pad upstairs. A nice cot. Nothing fancy. Just big enough for one. Let's make one, baby.'

He didn't move. She took his hand. He knew what this was, but let himself be drawn to the door.

As soon as they stepped inside he shoved her headlong and ducked low. Something whistled past his ear. He turned and kicked and chopped and jabbed and didn't stop even when the shape thudded to the floor. Finally he backed into the open door. 'Infant, come here.'

The girl was standing about fifteen feet away, near a

93

wrecked staircase that went up eight or ten steps and ended in empty space. 'You gonna hit me? If you gonna hit me, I'm gonna mark you good.'

'I'm not going to hit you. I want you to strike a match and see how your friend is doing.'

She came across the floor, trash and debris crunching under her shoes. She fumbled in her blouse pocket, struck a match and bent low.

The man was Negro and broad and of an indeterminate age – indeterminate because his features were hidden by blood.

The match went out. Another flared, but no longer near the man. The girl was lighting a cigarette. 'Maybe he's dead,' she said.

'Why don't you find out?'

'Not me. I don't want to know. He had this great big idea. It worked maybe three, four times, but he got all the bread and all I got was his two hundred pounds.'

Ted turned to go.

'Hey, wait. Let's make it. Five dollars.' She came to him. 'You can pay after.'

Ted laughed and let himself be drawn back inside. He said, 'Don't tell me you can fly. It'll take wings to get up those stairs.'

'We don't need upstairs. We don't need nothin' but here.' She closed the door and stepped on her cigarette. It was very dark and very quiet. He heard the man's breath – a sick, bubbling, sucking sound.

'How do you know I'll pay you after?'

She backed up slowly, drawing him along with her, until they were some ten feet from where the man lay.

'There's nothing you can do if I don't.'

'That's right.' She was up against the wall. 'I'll take a chance. I need bread bad. And what I got to lose?'

She leaned against the wall and did things to her clothing and did things to him, and then he was engulfed in warmth. One of her legs went up and around his waist and she whispered, 'Give baby her bottle, daddy,' and he couldn't hold back and he hoped there were no other friends around. He took her firm, round bottom in both hands and was swallowed by sweetness.

94

Later she smoked a cigarette and watched as he struck matches and examined the man. He looked up. 'He's badly hurt, infant. You'd better get him to a doctor.'

'Yeah.'

He went to her and took out his wallet. He told her to light a match, and he found a five and gave it to her.

'See?' she said, triumphant. 'I don't hafta hit people on the head. It was real good, wasn't it?'

He went to the door. 'It was.'

'And I only been practicin' two years,' she said, and laughed hard – a rollicking belly laugh that filled the dead house and drowned out the beaten man's breath and made Ted envy her driving, urgent sense of life.

He walked back east and caught a cab on Eighth Avenue. At home he showered and fell into bed and thought how good it would be if he could feel this empty, this drained, every night. He didn't fall asleep, but rather he passed out.

CHAPTER THIRTEEN

He was awake at nine. He lay in bed awhile, thinking of D'Andrea and the old man, but he didn't call Central Homicide. The lieutenant would let him know if anything happened.

He had the whole day to himself – ten or more hours until nightfall, when he would again set himself out as bait for the boy. Until then, he would do only pleasant things.

He could visit the office. He could go to the Metropolitan Museum of Art. He could rent a car and drive out to the shore.

He took his time showering and shaving, deciding what to do. He put on a lean, stylish, olive-green summer suit, a white button-down-collar shirt and a bright, yellow-and-brown striped tie. He left the apartment, walked two blocks, entered a shine stand and emerged with his black loafers gleaming. He crossed Second Avenue to a good luncheonette – almost empty now that it was ten fifteen – and sat in a booth and had coffee and eggs and toast with jelly and more coffee. At a quarter to eleven, he walked out and over to Third. At five after eleven he entered the block-square building that was finished in black stone and dark-tinted glass and took the first bank of elevators to the 18th floor.

Heavy, gilt lettering on a mahogany background read, 'Drizer Chemicals, Inc.' Smaller letters underneath advised that this floor belonged to Public Relations. He walked past the sign and pushed open the glass door to the reception room; the room was cool in pastel blues and grays as well as refrigerated air. Miss Ralerton rose from her desk with a light, girlish movement despite her fifty-odd years and considerable bulk. 'Mr Barth! How *nice* to see you again, Mr Barth. It must be all of six months since we last saw you. At least it *seems* that long.'

He nodded, even though it was close to ten months since he had set foot in this room and he had thought she would know it.

'And how *well* you look,' she sang. Miss Ralerton never

spoke; her voice was high and sweet and touched with Southern grace, and she lilted and trilled, but never just spoke. He had always thought her rather charming, but now her professional high spirits bothered him.

'Thank you. You're looking well too. Is Mr Powell in?'

'Yes he is, Mr Barth. I saw him only a few minutes ago, returning to his office from upstairs. Do you have an appointment?'

'No, just thought I'd drop in and say hello.'

'Oh. Well, I'm *sure* it's all right.' She picked up her phone and dialed the switchboard. 'We've all wanted to see you and say ...' She stopped to speak into the phone. 'Mr Powell's office, please, Alice.' She smiled at Ted without actually seeing him, and said, 'Is he available, Tess? Mr Barth is here to see him. Wait, you didn't know Mr Barth. Tell him Ted Barth is here, Tess. I just *know* he'll want to see him. Yes, yes, I'll hold.' Again the bright, unseeing smile.

Ted turned to the wall, where a series of Drizer products were mounted in shadow boxes: vitamin pills, topical ointments, several ethical drugs – just a few of more than 200.

Miss Ralerton said, 'Fine, Tess,' and then, 'He's *most* anxious to see you, Mr Barth.'

Ted started past her to the inner hallway. She said, voice soft, 'We were most grieved to hear the sad news, Mr Barth.'

He had to stop.

'But life must go on. I was simply prostrate after the death of my mother, but the Reverend Cherril said, "Life goes on, Miss Ralerton. Weep we may, but live we *must*." '

He nodded, a stiff smile on his lips, and continued into the hallway.

'Try to remember those words, Mr Barth,' she called after him. 'They will comfort you.'

He put his head down and walked quickly.

Someone called his name, and he waved into a doorway and went on without knowing who it was. He was passing through the ethical department. He turned a corner and was in the consumer-goods department. He didn't have to go very far, because at the end of a short corridor was Cort Powell's big office. The door was closed. Beside it, in a tiny recess, sat the latest in Cort's long line of exotic secretaries.

Ted said, 'I'm Mr Barth.'

'Yes, Mr Barth. He won't be a minute.' She smiled, and Ted found himself responding. It wasn't hard to respond to a Cort Powell secretary. He chose them carefully, much more carefully than he chose his writers. He had interviewed close to a hundred girls before picking Marjorie, the one who had been here in November. And at least as many before picking the spectacular redhead before Marjorie. He'd had six or seven secretaries in the eight years Ted had worked for him, and every one had been something to look at. Not just pretty – pretty girls were easy enough to find, since Cort paid well – but *different*. *Exotic*, as Cort himself classified them.

This one was blond, with what was almost a Buster Brown haircut. Her eyes were gray and were made dramatic by green eyeshadow. She wore pale pink lipstick.

Cort's door opened and an elderly man emerged. The secretary rose to escort him back to the reception room. She had a lean figure that swelled dramatically in the bottom. Her dress was green, a clinging, knitted shift, short and sleeveless. Her high-heeled shoes were green suede, her legs muscular and exciting in black, figured-lace stockings. He watched her as Cort came up and took his arm.

'Nice?'

Ted nodded.

'Glad to see you're looking again.'

'I never stopped,' Ted said, and followed Cort into the office. The department head went behind his curved Danish desk and Ted took a corner of the wall length, black couch.

'Want a job?'

'Just like that?' Ted said, smiling.

'I need a right-hand man. Perod's leaving industry for the glamour of a PR shop. I doubt if he's getting two grand more, the idiot. You can have what you were making when you left. Twenty-five. A deal?'

Ted shook his head. 'I can't. Later, maybe, when things clear up.'

'Later, maybe, when things clear up, I won't have the opening. It's been a year, hasn't it?'

'Nine months.'

'You can't cry forever. It was rough, no doubt about it, but now it's time to get back to work.'

Ted began to resent the glibness, the slick verbal approach and solution to a horror beyond Cort's understanding. He began to resent Cort himself – the tall, stooped, darkly elegant man who had the theatrically long hair and affected piercing eyes. As with Miss Ralerton, he no longer enjoyed the performance.

He stood up. 'Mind if I stroll around on my own?'

'Go ahead. Get the feel of a vital, exciting way of life again. Then come back and we'll talk some more.'

Ted nodded, but he wasn't coming back. He walked out and smiled at the secretary. 'You're the best yet.'

The girl returned his smile. 'But can I type?'

He would have stayed around and chatted, but it was too close to Cort. Besides, he wanted to see Susan. Susan who wasn't exotic. Susan who couldn't stop traffic the way this wild number could.

On the way he passed his old office, also a corner as befitted the second highest-paid writer at Drizer. The nameplate read 'Mr Perod' – the man who was leaving for greener pastures. It was empty, both desk lamp and ceiling light off, and he paused in the doorway and remembered working at that same desk, staring out those windows in search of ideas, or escape.

He remembered clearly how often he had sought escape. And then the memory slipped away and he remembered only working and lunching and rushing about in the controlled insanity of an executive-level PR man.

A thin little girl walked by and he recognized her as one of the secretaries. He said hello and she looked at him and said, 'Mr Barth! Hello!' He asked if Perod was in and she said no, he had called in sick but everyone knew he was goofing off because he was leaving next week. Ted thanked her and waited until she had gone, then entered the office and closed the door. He went to the desk, sat down and turned to the typewriter. His old typewriter. His old chair and desk and couch and green carpeting. Everything the way he had left it, including his white vase filled with long-stalked, multi-colored wheat. He should have felt perfectly at home.

He didn't. He felt tense, uneasy.

He left the corner office and walked down the hall and reached the bullpen area shared by trainees, juniors, traffic and media. Susan was there, across the jumble of desks and typing tables, and he weaved his way toward her. Several people said hello and he nodded and answered, but he was watching Susan. She looked up from her desk when he was still fifteen feet away, and he smiled and waved his hand. It was wonderful to see her.

'Well,' she said, leaning back in her chair, 'you're looking like a day on the town.'

'Dropped in to see Cort Powell.'

'Are you coming back to work?'

'Not yet.'

Her phone rang. She said, 'Excuse me, but it *is* a business day,' and picked up the handset. 'Shore, Public Relations.' The call wasn't business. He knew that as soon as her face and voice changed. She half-turned away from him and murmured, 'Yes, I am looking forward to it. Well, I'm not exactly free at the moment. Can I call you back? Oh, at school? Then wait a minute.' She covered the mouthpiece and turned back to Ted. 'I'm sorry, but I'm *so* busy right now. Nice of you to drop in, and I'll see you Sunday.' She waited for him to leave.

He chuckled and nodded and walked away, waving and looking around and greeting people. He left the bullpen and glanced back and felt pain. Susan was leaning on the desk, smiling into the phone.

Smiling at Arthur. Arthur who had called from school. Arthur who wanted to know if she was looking forward to tomorrow night. Arthur who was taking her from him.

The pain increased but it didn't get out of hand. It wasn't the pain a man felt at a hopeless situation. Because he would change the situation. He would remove Arthur. He would do it tomorrow night.

The decision made, he walked back to Cort's office, but not to see Cort.

The secretary greeted him. He said, 'Tess ... that *is* your name? How about dinner tonight?'

She raised her left hand and showed him the ring – a thin band of what looked like black plastic.

'Is that important?'

'Very,' she said, smiling.

There had been too much rejection today. 'Then why the *outré* costume? Why the billboard advertisement of sex?'

Her smile died. 'Goodbye, Mr Barth.'

He went back to the reception room and past Miss Ralerton's desk. She began to speak to him, but he didn't stop; he just went on out to the elevators and pressed the down button and stood with his back to Drizer Chemical.

The elevator came and he got inside, and a tall, thin VP named Barton was there. 'Ted, for the love of . . . when did you get back?'

'I'm not back,' he said flatly.

'Then where are you located?'

'Nowhere.'

The man hesitated. 'Well, how about lunch one day?'

'Why?' he said, and the elevator stopped and he walked out.

He heard the startled laugh and felt a hand on his arm. 'Listen, Ted, there's a little bar over east with some swinging waitresses . . .'

Redness was swallowing him. The urge to strike out and hurt and kill was swallowing him. He turned and said, 'Go away.'

Barton's mouth fell open.

'Go away before I smash your foolish face.'

Barton's mouth closed with a snap and he said, 'I heard about your trouble. I didn't hear you'd lost your mind.'

Ted's hand shot out – palm up, fingers stiff – and plunged deep into the soft spot beneath the man's ribs. Barton jack-knifed and spewed vomit. Ted walked away. He reached the street and it was almost twelve and hot and crowded and he bumped into people and sweated and snarled under his breath.

And knew he had to get off by himself somewhere.

He cut east to First Avenue, a more residential street and so less crowded. He found a bar, went inside and took a booth. He ordered a martini on the rocks and smoked and didn't look at the other people. He looked at the table, and when his drink came, he looked into the glass.

He sat drinking for three hours. He could barely walk

101

when he decided on what to do. Get a woman. A sure thing. A roll in the hay to wipe away the redness, the pain. A sure cure.

He went to the phone in the rear and closed the door and reached with thick fingers into his pocket. It took him some time to find a dime, and by then a heavyset man was standing outside, looking in at him with ill-concealed impatience. He opened the door and said, 'I'm going to be hours, buddy. I'm going to be all day. Try the drugstore on the corner.'

The heavyset man said, 'If you weren't so gassed . . .'

Ted came out of the booth, knowing he had to be fast; he crouched and coiled and concentrated hard on a single line of attack. But the man paled and walked quickly away and said something to the bartender as he left. The bartender looked at Ted. Ted smiled and nodded, as if agreeing with the bartender, and reentered the booth. He looked for his dime and found it on the ledge near the phone and took out his wallet and his address book. He peered owlishly at the pages, and laughed at himself, and suddenly laughed louder. He felt fine. By God, he would stay stoned . . .

But there was the boy. He would have to be perfectly sober to face the boy and his knife. Or he'd end up with Myra and Debbie.

'Won't think of that,' he muttered. He felt too good to think of that. And he was calling someone who would cancel out all of today's rejections. Edith Collers. Edith whom he'd had a month ago and who had called him several times afterward and whom he had brushed off because it wasn't Edith Collers and her big thighs and her big rear and her big breasts and her middle-aged anxiety – her desperate hunger for sex and for marriage – that he wanted. It was Susan. Cool Susan. Young, beautiful, cool Susan.

'After tomorrow night,' he muttered, and found the number and dropped the dime in the slot and dialed. 'After tomorrow night, but tonight I ball.'

No one answered, but he checked his watch and saw it was three fifteen and remembered that he had her office number too. Edith was a script consultant for one of the TV networks. Edith was a highly paid career gal of thirty-five or -six who wanted to be a lowly housewife.

After hanging up and reclaiming his dime, he checked his

book again and found her office number. He dialed and asked for Edith and waited; and then she was there and he said, 'Hey, this is Ted Barth – you busy after work? I was thinking we'd have a few drinks and a few laughs.'

'Well, hello,' she said, trying to sound cold.

'Yeah, hello.'

'I thought I'd heard the last of you.'

'No, not me. I always come back for more goodies. You haven't run out of goodies, have you?'

She laughed a little and said, 'I'm afraid not, though I'm dieting like crazy.'

'Well don't you dare reduce that lovely bumper. I've been thinking . . .'

'Where do you want to meet?' she asked, and added in a whisper, 'We can talk about that later.'

He said, 'Hold on a minute,' and went out to the bar. 'What d'you call this place?' he asked the bartender.

The man said, 'Four-Four Spot, because of the address.'

Ted went back to the booth and told Edith the address. She said she would be there at six or six thirty. He said, 'Better come right after work. I might not be here at six or six thirty.'

'Have you been drinking?'

'Oh mother, have I ever.'

'I'd like to freshen up and change . . .'

'You can freshen up at my place. Come quick. Oke?'

She said all right and he sent her a kiss and she said, 'You need someone to look after you, Ted Barth. It's time to straighten out. Life must go on.'

'To coin a phrase,' he said, and hung up.

He went back to his booth. He had half a martini waiting. He lit a cigarette and raised his glass and sipped. He looked into it. He waited for Edith Collers and her big thighs and her big rear and her big breasts.

Edith Collers' big thighs and big rear and big breasts were waiting for him when he came out of the bathroom. She had opened the sleeper couch and undressed and stretched out on her side. He said, 'That's what I call a good girl,' and went to her and fell on her and tried to get all of her in his hands. 'I'm going to enjoy this,' he kept whispering. 'Oh, baby, am I going to enjoy this.'

103

He didn't enjoy it. He worked at it and worked at it and after a while she knew something was wrong and murmured, 'What's the matter?' He didn't stop. He went on, fighting to finish. And finally he did and rolled away from her and lay on his face, gasping, unsatisfied and upset and unable to look at her.

She touched his shoulder. 'Ted, honey, what's the matter?'

'Too much liquor,' he said, and knew that was only a small part of it, if it was any part at all. Maybe the 'infant' last night had done a better job than he had realized.

But he didn't think that was it either. He had wanted a woman today – wanted one badly.

Edith got up and went to the armchair and began dressing. 'You can't even look at me,' she whispered thickly. 'All you wanted ...'

'I'm sorry,' he muttered – and he was. She had big breasts and big thighs and a big bottom and he had wanted to enjoy her, but he hadn't. He was sorry. He was sorry she had felt his lack of excitement.

'I ... cheapened myself for you,' she said. 'I knew what you'd suffered and I wanted to help. And how do you thank me? By drinking yourself into a ... a revolting stupor!'

She was saving face now. She was giving herself reasons for his lack of feeling for her. He raised his head and said, 'You're right, forgive me,' and let his head fall again and mumbled and acted much drunker than he was. He kept it up until after she had left. And by then something else had occurred to him.

Their mating had lacked ... violence. Last night he had fought and then loved, and it had been good. The first time with Edith he had not known until the very moment of capitulation whether she would actually go all the way. That too was a kind of violence – the violence of seduction. With the two professionals, the good part had come when Maxine had fought him. And it was a battle every moment with Susan – a battle to make her care.

He got up. He was giving it too much thought. It didn't deserve so much thought. He'd had a bad piece. So it was the first time since November that had happened. How many times with Myra ...

104

Guilt, goddam guilt! But once the boy was caught, it would all end.

He took a shower and made the water progressively colder until he was shivering beneath an icy jet. He stood there as long as he could, and when he got out, his head was clearer. He ate a sandwich and a can of peaches and drank a full container of orange juice.

It was seven ten. It wouldn't be dark for another hour and a half, and the streets wouldn't begin to empty for three or four hours. The boy wasn't likely to attack before midnight or later.

CHAPTER FOURTEEN

He set the alarm clock for twelve thirty and lay down.

The phone woke him. He squinted at the luminous hands of the clock. It was eleven. His mouth was dry. He had a slight headache. Not too bad after all he had drunk.

He lifted the phone and said, 'Yes?'

There was silence. He sat up, fully awake. The fogged, disguised, whispering voice said, 'I told you. I won't let you do it to me.'

'Who is this?' he said, keeping his voice clear.

'You know. I won't let you put me in the chair. I'll kill you first. I'm warning you, Barth. I won't burn. I'm warning you.'

'If you didn't do anything, you have nothing to worry about.' He was proud of the calm way he spoke. 'If you want to talk to me, why don't you come here? Drop over right now. Tell me what happened that night.'

Silence.

'It's one way to prove you didn't . . . hurt my wife and my daughter.' His need to kill the boy had almost torn loose then; he'd had to shove it down with every ounce of will power. 'I'm alone here. Come on over.'

'Sure, so the cops can get me. I won't let them get me. I won't let you put me in the chair.'

'I didn't tell them about your letter,' Ted said, and he was dripping sweat. 'I didn't tell them about yesterday's call. I was hoping you could come over and explain what happened and who could have done it if you didn't.'

Silence. And heavy breathing. And then, 'I don't know what happened. Just forget me. That's the only way. Forget me.'

'No, I can never forget you,' Ted said, and now he too was whispering – and now he was letting go. Holding back hadn't worked; letting go might. 'No, I'm going to watch you die soon. They got the old man. Did you know that? They got Abel and he'll tell who you are and then I'll pick you out of a lineup and they'll put you in the chair and you'll scream and you'll die and I'll stand there laughing in your face – laughing in your filthy face because I know you, don't forget that I know you, I saw you with your brown hair and your filthy face, and I'll say that's him, take him and burn him ...'

'I'll kill you!' the voice screamed, and the line went dead.

That scream had been undisguised and full of fear. The boy would come – tonight, if he gave him the chance.

He got up, rubbing his hands together and chewing his lip and whispering, 'Please, please,' like a prayer for love or health or success ... but it was a prayer for death, for the chance to pit his hands against the boy's knife.

As he dressed he thought, 'What if he has a gun?' For something this important the boy might buy a gun. His hands would be no good against a gun.

It stopped him. It made him consider buying a gun of his own. But then he couldn't hold to the thought, couldn't change his plan – his need to tear the boy into bloody fragments with his bare hands, to turn loose everything he'd learned in the *dojo* and on the streets in one carnival of carnage, in one red finish to the redness.

For that he would risk anything.

He finished dressing and wondered why D'Andrea hadn't called him, or whether he might have called earlier in the day. That old man should have cracked by now.

He dialed Central Homicide and got D'Andrea. He asked about the old man.

'Yeah, well, we had sort of a bad break,' the lieutenant said heavily. 'He killed himself a few hours ago. You won't believe it if I tell you how.'

'Try me,' Ted muttered, the heaviness transferred to him. (God, God, now it might never end.)

'He was close to cracking. He begged me to let him sleep a few hours, but I kept after him. He passed out and I figured maybe he'd die on us so I got a doctor. The doctor wanted to transfer him to a hospital, but I told him the score and he said I could keep him one more day. Just one more day. Believe me, I had someone watching him every minute. He went back to his cell for a few hours' sleep, which was more than I'd had since we'd picked him up. I lay down upstairs and the next thing I knew he was dead. The man on duty never had a chance to spot it. If he'd tried to hang himself or cut himself, he'd never have made it. You won't believe what he did, the poor bastard.'

Ted waited.

'He took off his shirt and stuffed a sleeve down his throat. Strangled on it. Held it down and died with hardly a sound. Even so, the guard heard something and came over. But it was too late. Choked himself to death lying there. Lucky we booked him after you left. Damn lucky, or my ass would be in one big sling.'

'So we're back where we started.'

'Don't you believe it. One of the tenants saw the old man drinking with a boy about two weeks ago. Not in the house. In a bar about four blocks away. No one else ever saw the kid, so I guess he's not a relative.'

'He must've meant plenty to the old man,' Ted said, 'or else why would he kill himself rather than talk?'

'You're assuming a lot. That old man was sick and desperate. He knew he'd never get out of jail – not with *his* record. He was also a user, an addict. He couldn't face life in a cell. So he ended it. With his prospects, I'd have done the same.'

'How can you find the boy?'

'The bartender says the old man drank there half a dozen times with the kid. We've got a detail covering the place every minute it's open. We're going to find someone who knows that boy.'

'Now you're assuming a lot ... that it's the same boy we're looking for.'

'Yes, but the odds are with us.'

Ted was silent.

'Anything unusual happen?' the lieutenant asked.

'Like what?'

'Threatening phone calls? Someone following you? What we once talked about.'

'No. You're going to have to do it the hard way.'

It was the lieutenant's turn to be silent.

'Will it become public knowledge that Abel died?'

'We're ahead of you there. He's at the city morgue. He's listed as an unidentified body. He'll stay that way as long as

108

we can put off his wife. Which won't be longer than this one night.'

'Great,' Ted whispered bitterly. 'Great.'

'We'll get him,' D'Andrea said. 'Don't doubt that for a minute.'

'You said something like that nine months ago.'

'It still holds true. Meanwhile the boy doesn't know Abel's dead. He's just liable to do something stupid. Maybe even come in here and give himself up. Or talk to a priest, a minister or a rabbi, who'll talk him into giving himself up. Or tell his mother or his girl, who'll talk him into giving himself up.' He chuckled. 'Any one of a dozen good people can help us put that kid in the chair.'

Ted said yeah and good night and hung up. His headache had grown worse. He wanted to take one of the sleeping pills – the only thing that did the job – but he couldn't afford the loss of perception, of hair-trigger reaction.

He took four aspirin and went out. He began to walk. It was Friday night, with the weekend ahead, and New York was up late. He kept walking. He went over toward the West Side, toward the jungle. More people. Broadway was Coney Island. More and more people. He kept going – Eighth Avenue, Ninth Avenue – and the streets grew poor and dark, and the people grew shabby and the kids grew tough. They sat on stoops, or leaned against walls and cars, or stood in doorways. It was a hot, close night. The jungle was wide awake. Too many people.

And yet something began to happen; a feeling took hold of him.

As he approached the massive shadow that was the West Side Elevated Highway, as he smelled the dank heaviness of the Hudson River, he suddenly knew he was being followed. The urge to turn and look was immediate and powerful but he resisted it. He kept walking.

Without proof, with no way of knowing, he knew that the boy was somewhere behind him.

He had to turn, finally, under the elevated, and here there was only a scattering of people, and one was a cop, and he glanced to the right as he walked uptown and he saw no one who could have been the boy. But there was darkness everywhere and deep shadows everywhere and he knew ... he knew. He walked on – with the tension mounting and the need mounting – and he prayed, 'Please, please.'

He searched for dark streets, empty streets. He went to streets of warehouses, of closed businesses, and even here were people, escaping their broiling tenements, their close and crowded rooms.

He reached Broadway and walked to a movie house and stood looking at the stills, then bought a ticket and went inside. He paused at the candy stand, in line with the ticket taker's open door, in full view of the street. He bought a chocolate bar and moved slowly away. An usher showed him down the center aisle, waiting for him to make a choice. It was chilly and two-thirds empty. He took a seat up front with three or four totally empty rows behind him. He crossed his legs and looked at the screen and tried to hear over the sound track. He waited for someone to enter the row behind him.

Time passed. He ate the candy bar and wanted a drink of water. But he gave it more time. Finally, he heard movement behind him and tried to stay loose and uncrossed his legs and felt his neck stiffen. Something touched the back of his seat; he jerked his head to the right and followed with his body and turned, crouching behind the seats. The startled faces of a middle-aged man and woman gaped at him. He straightened and smiled apologetically and walked to the aisle. He went to the back – to the water fountain – and saw a boy who had been standing off to the side, leaning on the half-wall and looking at the screen. He saw this boy move quickly down the side aisle and take a seat and slump low. A boy with strange hair. He couldn't be sure in the half-light, but it had looked red. Carroty-red.

He drank, then turned and saw the sign for the rest rooms. He walked to a staircase and down it and into a small waiting room with three chairs and a couch and two doors, one reading, 'Men'. Inside a thin boy of twelve or thirteen stood at one of the two urinals; an older man washed his hands at the single sink and said, 'If your mother gets angry about my keeping you out this late, say I was making up for last Sunday. She kept you at that family dinner till five thirty, and I'm supposed to have you every Sunday, a *full* day.'

The boy finished at the urinal and flushed it and glanced

at Ted, who went to a scale and searched his pockets for a penny. 'All right,' the boy muttered, and his face was a sad boy's face. Ted knew what he was feeling and wanted to go to the father and shake him and tell him, 'Look what you're doing to the boy. Look what your wife, or ex-wife, is doing to the boy.'

'Remember,' the father said, 'it's my right.'

The boy nodded and washed his hands.

Ted put a penny in the slot and stepped on the scale. One seventy-three. He had gained three pounds since he had last weighed himself. And when had that been? At the doctor's office a few days ago. But he had been stripped then, so his weight had probably stayed the same.

'Don't let her change your mind about things,' the father said. 'She cries when she wants to, you know. Turns it on like a faucet. One time she made me drive all the way . . .'

They went out, the boy's head down, the man's face flushed with angry memories. Ted had no time for memories, but the look and sound of that particular kind of anger brought back scenes in his Brooklyn home twenty or more years ago, when his mother and father tore at each other. It made his headache worse.

He went to the sink, washed his hands and glanced at the two booths. Both were open and empty. He used the roller towel, then entered the booth nearest the sink and locked the door. He sat down and waited.

Someone came into the bathroom. Someone went over to the sink and turned on the water. Someone left the water on and moved softly to the booth and stood at the side. Someone with pointy-toed, black shoes.

Ted flushed the toilet, waited a minute, then opened the door, ready to spin left and lunge forward in a knife-disarming attack. But as he did, someone else came in. A red-headed boy ran from the room, knocking aside the elderly man who had entered. Ted ran after him because that red hair was wrong – garishly wrong. He ran as hard as he could, through the waiting room and up the stairs. He didn't see the boy and felt he had been tricked, so he went downstairs again. The elderly man was standing outside the men's room, gesticulating to another elderly man. He pointed at Ted. Ted looked at them and around the waiting room, and only then saw the door marked 'Emergency Exit'. He went to it and opened it and looked up a metal staircase. He climbed it, slowly now that he had no chance to catch the red-haired boy, and reached a hallway which led back to the theatre in one direction and to a double-door in the other direction. He went to the door, pushed down on the bar lever and came out on a side street, twenty-five or thirty feet from Broadway.

He walked home. He hadn't seen the redheaded boy's face, but he knew what it looked like – hard and challenging and murderous.

He left his door unlocked but had no hope the boy would come tonight. He no longer had much hope the boy would ever come, because he had been chased and frightened and forewarned. And the old man was dead and D'Andrea had so little to go on and this life would continue – this hopeless, ugly, ruined life would continue forever.

He couldn't sleep until he had promised himself he would do something to change this life. He couldn't sleep until he had reminded himself that tomorrow was Saturday and tomorrow night he would turn Susan from Arthur to himself. And even then he had to kill his headache with one of his sleeping pills. Even then it was drugs – and not peace – which brought him sleep.

CHAPTER FIFTEEN

He stood with his back against the padlocked gate, in the shadows of the alley across the street from Susan's apartment – the same spot he had stood in early Thursday morning.

It was almost two A.M. He had been there since a few minutes to twelve, Saturday night. But he had been waiting for Susan and Arthur far longer than that. He had been waiting all day.

He had slept late, deliberately going back to sleep after waking at ten. He had exercised with his weights for the first time in a week, and made it a real workout – from eleven thirty to almost one. Then he had showered and shaved and eaten, and had watched television until four. He had dressed and gone out to the supermarket and done a week's shopping. He had gone to the liquor store to stock up on bourbon and had treated himself to a bottle of Montrachet. He had read until eight and had made a more elaborate dinner than usual, drinking half the bottle of wine with his mutton chop. Two more hours of television had brought him to eleven twenty. The last thing he had done before leaving the apartment was to run through (with half-blows) three basic attacks he could use tonight. The choice would depend on Arthur's reactions to his opening gambit.

He had thought of the boy while walking uptown. He had tried a few dark side streets, but nothing had happened and he hadn't really expected anything to happen. He felt it was all up to D'Andrea now. He felt he had lost his personal chance at the boy; but that didn't mean he wasn't prepared to react if the boy appeared.

Even now, with his eyes watching the corner, with his ears straining for Susan's voice and laughter, he realized there were several other alleys along the block in which the boy could be hiding, and a dozen rooftops that would allow him to keep this particular alley under observation.

Anything was possible, but the probabilities kept him concentrating on Susan and Arthur.

A cab came around the corner and pulled to the curb. At first he couldn't see who got out because the cab itself blocked his view, but then it left and Arthur was putting his his wallet back in his pocket and Susan was touching her hair.

Ted released his breath, pent up for fear that Susan would emerge from the cab alone and that Arthur would continue on and out of reach. But of course that wouldn't happen. Arthur wasn't going to pass up a long good night. Not Arthur.

The redness came and he welcomed it. Now he began building up to the moment of release – of savage release and satisfaction. Now his hands stretched open and closed, stretched open and closed. Now his arm and shoulder muscles knotted.

He had to wait an interminable half hour more, at which time the husky, nineteen-year-old Hank Shore came around the corner, whistling shrilly. He kept up his whistling as he approached the street-level apartment and intensified it as he went to the door. A warning signal, no doubt.

Ted smiled thinly. *Oh, Arthur, poor Arthur, this night's pleasure is going to have to last a long time. This night's pleasure is going to have to be remembered for weeks in a hospital bed. At least a broken arm for poor Arthur, plus internal injuries. Perhaps a broken leg too, poor Arthur. And by the time you're ready to call on Susan again, she'll belong to Ted Barth. And if she doesn't yet belong to Ted Barth, then back to your hospital bed, poor Arthur, with further injuries. Poor, poor Arthur.*

He wouldn't worry about Susan's finding out who had injured poor Arthur. He would win his woman first, then worry. All's fair in love and war. Arthur would never in all his life need a woman as much as Ted Barth needed Susan. Arthur would go his handsome Ivy League way and find other women – many of them – and find *that one woman* years from now when he was ready to settle down. It wouldn't bother *him* much to lose Susan, but Susan was the one and only woman for Ted Barth.

Arthur came out of the shadows and onto the street and turned toward First Avenue. Ted moved quickly from the alleyway ... and almost stumbled, his legs heavy from the

114

inactivity of the past two hours, his head light – too light. He walked faster, his legs loosening rapidly. He moved his shoulders as he walked and rubbed the back of his neck, trying to shake the lightheadedness. He needed the weight of flesh, bone and reality to handle Arthur. He needed clarity and speed.

He hurried across the street, remembering how Arthur had escaped him the last time, determined to strike before it could happen again. He was only twenty-five or thirty feet from the tall boy and catching up rapidly. He would over-take him at the corner and fight him back onto 83rd Street where no one could interfere, at least not for the few minutes necessary to finish the job. But he still moved his shoulders and shook his head and felt the lightness, the dangerous vertigo of unreality. Then . . . he heard the third set of foot-steps.

He didn't want to hear them, didn't want to believe in them, didn't want to look. *Not now. Nothing must interfere now.*

He looked across the street where the footsteps clicked at a pace equal to his own, and his stride faltered. Was it his spinning brain? Was it a fantasy of his tortured mind? He had done so many stupid things lately, had tormented himself with so much unreality and had had so many nightmares in the past nine months. Could this be another, a more ad-vanced fantasy – one with sound and substance – intruding on his waking hours?

The man he saw was young; he could tell that from his walk, his carriage, his body structure – even though that body was camouflaged by a strange costume. He wore a long, gray, plastic raincoat that crinkled and glimmered in the light of a streetlamp, and a shabby, wide-brimmed hat – the kind seen in gangster films of the 1940's (it wasn't raining: why such a hat on a young man?) He strode along with his heels clicking on the pavement, his leather heels, the kind of heels that came with certain pointy-toed shoes worn by tough kids from tough neighborhoods. Pointy-toed shoes like the shoes outside the toilet booth in the movie house last night.

He couldn't shake the dizziness, the sense of unreality. His pace slowed as Arthur turned the corner and the man

115

across the street slowed up. Their footsteps moved together and Ted fought to wake up, to grasp certainty and purpose – but he couldn't.

Did that man have red hair? Unnatural carroty-red hair?

He reached the corner and turned after Arthur, who was halfway down the block now; but he didn't hurry after him. The footsteps behind him deadened, and he knew the man had stepped into the gutter and was crossing on the softer surface of blacktop. He walked after Arthur, no longer chasing him. He walked with his brain spinning and his body not yet ready because he couldn't adjust, couldn't decide, couldn't wake up from the fog of unreality.

The footsteps again clicked behind him. They didn't hurry – they just kept pace with him.

He reached the corner and Arthur was a long way down the next block. He turned left, leaving Arthur – turned into 82nd Street and the darkness and the quiet of sleeping apartment houses. He walked slowly and the footsteps seemed to hesitate; then they came after him, and came quickly. He put his head down and told himself he was being followed and that under the raincoat was a boy's body and under the ridiculous wide-brimmed hat was carroty-red hair and a hard, challenging face. And still he couldn't wake and still he moved without purpose and still he rambled in his thoughts between Susan and Arthur and Edith Collers and his fantasies and his nightmares. And finally the rambling reached the boy. And finally he was able to stop at the boy. And finally he drew a deep breath and his body tightened. Finally ... when it was almost too late.

The sharp, clicking sound had stopped. He hadn't realized it, but it had stopped some seconds ago.

Sudden sixth-sense warning screamed an alert and he jerked his head around. The ridiculous, flapping figure was almost on him, racing along on its toes, body held high and right arm held high, leaning forward like a flamenco dancer in climactic approach to the female. The raised right hand glinted a long extension. The raised right hand held thin, sharp death.

He screamed the *keeyi*, freed at last of rules, freed at last

116

of every vestige of restraint. Now he wouldn't have to remind himself to strike not-too-hard at not-too-vital spots. Now he wouldn't have to worry where his kicks landed, or whether they killed. Now his hands could create the redness they had lusted after for nine, almost ten months. Now, this instant, not some yearned-for tomorrow. *Now!*

The *keeyi*'s shrill power struck the raincoated figure and made it falter – just for a split second but that was long enough. The knife came down and Ted was leaning to the right and the knife missed his chest and touched his shoulder. There was a sharp, quick burn, but he forgot it. The figure's hat fell off as he staggered past, and the hair was red – carroty red, freshly dyed red – and the twisted, grimacing face was the boy's face, and it wasn't a fantasy. It was real! Ted kicked out with his right foot and struck the boy's shin. His shoe scraped down, tearing thin flesh pinned against rigid bone. The boy wailed and turned, hopping momentarily in agony, and then went low and held the knife low and far out to the right.

Ted circled him. The boy hobbled a bit but turned with him. He knew how to use that knife. He had learned in the streets and he had learned well. Ted moved in, feinting, and the knife flashed in, feinting; and then they were back to circling each other.

The boy stepped back suddenly, trying to shake off the open raincoat, but Ted was in just as suddenly, left hand out and stabbing for the eyes, right hand up like a hatchet, ready to chop. The boy went back into defensive position and remained encumbered by flapping plastic.

Ted heard the car but never took his eyes from the boy. The boy glanced to the left, and that was all the chance Ted needed. He came in so low his fingers scraped the pavement, and came up as the boy's eyes and knife snapped toward him. He screamed the *keeyi*, triumphantly now that his left hand had grasped the knife wrist and arrested its forward momentum. It was over. In a moment the boy would be shrieking, but the sound would be weak and wet. In a moment his throat would be crushed by a powerful hand chop, and before he died of that, his testes would be crushed, and before he fainted of that, his intestines would be

117

smashed, and only then would the throat be finished, the vile life finished, the searching and the agony finished.

He threw him with a simple *harai goshi*, but gave the sweeping hip throw enormous force and held to the knife wrist and felt it wrench from its socket. The boy shrieked; the knife clattered on the pavement. Shriek Number One, Ted thought, his right hand starting down.

It never completed the chop. It was grabbed from behind and yanked back. He was pulled off balance and a voice said, 'That's enough, Mr Barth. We've got him. That's enough.'

But it wasn't enough. They couldn't stop him. It was only the first shriek. There were more to come. There was the last wet, weak shriek to come.

He regained his balance and prepared for his escape move, an over-the-shoulder throw. But a tall, heavyset man in a gray suit stepped in front of him, a gun in his hand, and said, 'Easy, Mr Barth. We know. But we can't let you do it.' He glanced at the boy, who was clutching his right wrist and writhing on the pavement, then back to Ted. 'You understand, don't you? D'Andrea had us tailing you since Abel Warner died. He figured you'd be baiting this one. We were almost too slow as it was.'

'Please,' Ted whispered. 'Just walk away for a minute. Just to the corner and back.'

'You'd better cuff him,' the detective in gray said to the man holding Ted.

'Please,' Ted whispered.

His hands were cuffed behind him. The man who did it held his arm and stepped around front. He was another big detective, wearing brown instead of gray. He said, 'It's over, Mr Barth. I'll take the cuffs off soon as you settle down. We'd like to let you do it, but we can't.' He looked down at the boy and his face grew hard. 'I'd like to help you do it.'

The boy looked up then. He looked at Ted and he was crying and he said, 'You're not going to do it to me. You bastard, you're not . . .'

The detective in gray slapped him across the ear, a heavy slap with a heavy hand. 'You'll get your chance to talk soon. Till then, shut up.'

Ted turned away. He was empty now, he told himself.

But in the car, sitting alone in back while the boy sat up front between the two detectives, he began to sweat. 'Now the lawyers will start,' he said.

The boy wept steadily.

'Now they'll say he's a child and too young to die and capital punishment is wrong. Now they'll listen to his lies, all the lies he'll make up to save his life.'

'Not this case,' the detective in brown said. He drove swiftly, siren wailing. 'Matt and me'll put the last nail in his coffin with our testimony. He tried to kill you. He tried to kill the eyewitness.'

'I didn't kill the others,' the boy wept. 'I never . . .'

Ted lunged forward, hands still cuffed, trying to butt the carroty-red head, seeing the beds and the blood all over and the hard face, the challenging face, in the doorway of the guest room.

They stopped and the detective in gray got in back with him and held him down and they drove on and he listened to the boy cry and he said, 'Just tell me, if you didn't do it who did?' He had to repeat it three times before the boy stopped crying and answered.

'I don't know. It wasn't me, that's all I know.'

'You were the one,' Ted said, and he made his voice quiet and he made his voice hard. 'I'll swear to that and they've got fingerprints and you tried to kill me.'

The boy said nothing.

'Tell me. It's not official unless you sign a confession, and even that isn't always official. Just tell me.'

The boy was silent.

'You were there. The fingerprints will prove . . .'

The boy turned his head. He and Ted looked at each other and Ted whispered, 'Yes, it was you.'

The boy said, 'I was there. It was me.'

The detective in gray said, 'That's the only way, kid. You tell that to Lieutenant D'Andrea and you'll feel better. Make your peace with God.'

'I was there. I'll tell that to anyone. I took the stuff and I gave it to Abel and he hocked it for me. But I never killed anyone.'

Ted spat at his face. The boy screamed, 'They kept saying

119

I killed them. In the papers they said the robber killed them. I never killed them.'

'Then who?' the detective who was driving said. 'There were two people left alive in that apartment, you and Mr Barth. You saying Mr Barth did it?'

'Don't guys kill their wives?' the boy shouted. The detective took one hand off the wheel and struck him and knocked him halfway down on the seat.

'Don't raise your voice anymore.'

The detective in gray leaned forward and helped the boy sit up straight. 'A wife, yes. But what you're saying is that this man killed his nine-year-old daughter.'

The boy began to cry again.

Ted leaned back and his eyes closed. He couldn't think now, but he promised himself he would think later. He would be seeing the boy again. He would get a chance at the boy again.

The detective in gray said, 'I guess we can take those cuffs off now, Mr Barth.' He unlocked them.

Ted massaged his arms. 'I'm glad you stopped me.'

The detective patted his knee. 'You're okay, Mr Barth. You're a man, and that's no shit.'

The boy wept. Ted and the detective talked. The detective asked him why he had staked himself out in that alley for two hours instead of walking around. Ted decided instantly that big lies were out; they might confuse the issue and help the boy in court. 'I know someone who lives across the way. The last time I was there, I thought I was being followed. So I decided to return and make out I was watching . . .' He waved his hand. 'I followed someone else, hoping the boy would follow me.'

'That tall kid who came with the girl?'

'Yes. I know the girl.'

The detective glanced at him. 'Two birds with one stone?'

'Not really, but it's all right if you think so.'

The detective shrugged. 'Your personal life's your own. Nothing changes what we know about this punk. If the fingerprints match, he's had it.'

'When do I get a lawyer?' the boy said, still crying. 'I wasn't even eighteen at the time.'

'It's starting,' Ted murmured.

The detectives said nothing.

'When do I get . . .' the boy began. The detective who was driving raised his arm. The boy ducked away and whispered, 'Okay, okay.'

They rode on in silence.

CHAPTER SIXTEEN

The boy's name was Andrew Bresk. He had lied in the car about not being eighteen at the time of the murders. He was almost nineteen now – old enough to burn for his crimes.

Ted learned this from Matt Oden, the detective in gray, who came to the room in back where Ted was being treated by a doctor. The doctor finished bandaging the two-inch cut on Ted's right shoulder – the cut that hadn't been noticed until they walked into the light of the station house – and said, 'The only real damage is to your suit. Five dollars, please.'

Ted said, 'I thought it was on New York's Finest.' Matt Oden grinned. The doctor pocketed his money and left. Ted leaned against the slatted back of the wooden bench and answered Oden's grin, but inside he wasn't grinning. Inside, nothing had changed. 'I'd like to be there when they question Bresk,' he said.

'They've been questioning him for twenty minutes already, and I don't think D'Andrea will let you. But I'll ask, if you want.'

'Yes, please.'

Oden lit a cigarette. 'Soon as I finish this.'

Ted lit one too. 'What about the fingerprints?'

'They'll match. The kid admits being in your apartment. He just won't say he killed anyone. Can't blame him there. No one wants to strap himself into the chair. He says he went for you because you were framing him.'

Ted threw down his cigarette.

'That shouldn't bother you, Mr Barth. They all squirm around when it's Murder One – first degree and a capital offense. And Bresk's got a record from the age of fourteen. Juvenile delinquency. Narcotics addiction. Assault on a teacher. Car theft, twice. Petty larceny, twice. Assault with a deadly weapon just two weeks before he broke into your place.'

'Then why was he walking the streets, free to kill my family?' His voice had risen, and he shook his head.

Oden looked at his cigarette. 'Yeah, why. Ask the judges. Ask the social welfare people. Ask the state psychiatrists. Ask anyone but the cops who push for stiff sentences.'

'I'd like to.'

'Anyway, his prints are on file. They're being compared with the prints from your apartment. The mobile crime lab was called and they're here right now. D'Andrea's not wasting a minute. He's going to sew it all up before sunrise.'

Ted remained grim.

Oden stood up. 'Listen, you got nothing to complain about. I mean, even if the kid gets life, even if he gets twenty years, you got nothing to cry about. You don't know – and I don't like to say – how many cases like this never get solved. Cases without motive. Hot prowl cases. Nut cases.' He went to the door. 'I'll ask the lieutenant if you can come in.'

Ted sat and waited. He told himself Oden was right. It was over and he had nothing to complain about.

Oden came back. 'It's okay, but only because they're almost finished. D'Andrea wants to talk to you.'

He followed the detective into the now-familiar, grim hallway and down it and through a door on the left just before the desk room. It was a big room, bare except for five round-bottomed, straight-backed chairs. Andrew Bresk sat slumped on one of the chairs, his head down, his hands limp on his lap, his back to the door. One wrist was heavily taped. He looked small and thin and weak compared with the heavyset men scattered around the room. There was D'Andrea in a chair facing Bresk, leaning forward with one big hand on the boy's knee. There was the detective in brown standing behind D'Andrea. There were two other detectives half-sitting on the sill of the room's single window. There was a patrolman sitting near the door. There was a middle-aged, balding man seated off to the right of Bresk, a man with a pad and pencil who wrote steadily. And there were Oden and Ted, himself. Ted felt that the boy was surrounded, overwhelmed, bound to be defeated in whatever defense maneuvers he might try.

But he hadn't confessed. That became evident immediately.

'So let's recap,' D'Andrea said, and glanced at the male stenographer. 'You had a fix the afternoon of November third. You were broke and couldn't raise any money and couldn't beg a fix from the third to the ninth. You'd been carrying a big monkey for almost a year – a fix a day, sometimes two. And here it was five days without anything but a few goofballs. And the sixth day came along and you were sick and you were wild . . .'

'I wasn't wild,' the boy whispered. 'I told you. I was able to go awhile then. I wasn't hooked like I am now. Honest, I was able to go awhile.'

'It's different now, huh? Now a day or two and you're in withdrawals?'

The boy nodded, head still down. 'If you could just call a doctor . . .'

'Sure. As soon as you tell us the truth.'

'I told you the truth,' the boy whispered, but he never looked up and he didn't seem to expect anyone to believe him and he didn't seem to believe himself.

'We're dancing in circles,' D'Andrea said, voice growing hard. 'You can't afford that, Bresk. Tonight, tomorrow, tomorrow night . . . no doctor and no lawyer. I can hold you a week if I want.'

The boy looked up, aghast. 'No you can't. Not a week. Maybe tonight and maybe tomorrow but not a week. You can't.'

D'Andrea leaned back. The detective in brown said, 'Remember the one we kept eight days? Cold turkey. Screaming so no one could . . .'

'No, no, no,' the boy whispered, and tears ran from his eyes and he began to shake.

'And the rape case we kept for six,' the patrolman at the door said. 'He was a two-a-dayer, like this one. The poor bastard didn't confess until he was half nuts. Could've saved himself from the looney bin.'

'And the Brown brothers,' Matt Oden said from where he and Ted stood on the other side of the door from the patrolman. 'Two days. Screaming and begging for shoe-laces, bedding, anything to finish themselves off. And all they had to do was tell the truth, which they did. Then we got them a doctor and he gave them a shot – something to ease the withdrawals – and they got the same stuff every day, right until the trial. Even afterward.'

124

'Even the day they got burned,' the boy said, and hugged himself to stop the trembling.

'They didn't burn,' Oden said flatly. 'All they did was kill a cop. He was a real brute. They got twenty years to life. Just about what you'll get, if you cooperate.'

Ted jerked forward. Oden put a hand on his arm and shook his head.

The boy said, 'I didn't do it. I want to call my brother.'

'So let's see then. You were five full days without a fix. You started out the afternoon of November ninth to get some dough. You were in bad shape.'

'I said I could go longer . . .' the boy began.

D'Andrea took his hand off the boy's knee and poked him under the chin with a stiff thumb. The boy's head jerked up. 'Time to listen,' D'Andrea said quietly. 'You want to talk, say what you did to that woman and girl. Otherwise, just listen.' He lowered his hand to Bresk's knee. Bresk's head dropped down again.

'You were in bad shape. And you didn't get anything in Central Park, where you went about six, hoping to catch some old lady on a path in the Ramble. You hung around the park until almost eight, when you left and started walking downtown along Lexington or Madison, you're not sure which. You stopped at a luncheonette – sounds like one on Lex near Grand Central – about nine and had coffee and chewed the wick of a benzedrine inhaler for a lift. You stayed there until after ten, then went back on the street. You picked up a girl near Thirty-fourth and Third and tried to con her into giving you some money and when she wouldn't you pulled her into a doorway and tried to take it from her. She yelled and there were people on the street and you had to run without her purse.

'At a little after midnight you were moving back uptown along First. You cut down a few streets looking for fire escapes, and on Fifty-fourth you came to the house the Barths lived in. You climbed the alley gate and pulled down the fire escape ladder . . .'

'It was almost all the way down,' the boy interrupted.

D'Andrea's hand left his knee.

'You want to keep it straight, don't you?' the boy said, leaning away.

D'Andrea's hand went back to the knee. 'The ladder was almost all the way down. You pulled it down a little more and climbed it and went up, looking into windows, trying to find a place that looked like the tenants weren't home. But it seemed everyone was home, and so you went all the way to the ninth floor, the top floor, and even here you didn't like the look of things. The lights were out, but there was a man's coat thrown over the couch in the living room – the room you could see – and other things, and you felt the place was occupied. But you couldn't wait any longer. You were wild.'

The boy's head came up. D'Andrea's hand lifted from the knee. The boy's head went down.

'You found the double window was latched shut. You worked at it. You dug at the wood with your knife, and it wasn't long, maybe five minutes, before you broke the latch and opened the window and climbed inside. You went to the end of the living room and looked right and saw the hall door and just before it the kitchen. You turned left, down a foyer, and passed an open door and saw a man sleeping and went on. You came to another room, a kid sleeping, and figured there wouldn't be much there – a kid's possessions – and went on. You came to a woman's room and she was sleeping and you just had to get some dough for a fix and you went in and you looked around and there wasn't anything and she woke up . . .'

'There *was* something,' the boy said. 'I told you, the ring was on the dresser. I took the ring off the dresser.'

D'Andrea's thumb poked into Bresk's chin. Bresk cried out and D'Andrea said, 'Now let's not waste any more time, boy. There's a shit storm coming your way and you know it. There's the withdrawals and the trial. There's death row and sweating out appeals. There's burning in the chair, if you don't cooperate. Let me tell you what happened, and then you'll sign and then we'll help you as best we can. Mr Barth said his wife slept with her rings on. You found nothing and she woke up and you panicked and used your knife. When it was over you pulled the ring off her finger. You went back down the hall to the kid's room. You were really gone now. You'd killed and you were wild and you didn't care. You looked through the kid's stuff and she woke up and you had

126

nothing to lose and you shut her up the same way you shut up the woman. With your knife.'

The boy made a choking sound. D'Andrea waited. The boy said nothing.

'You found the recorder in the kid's room, in the closet along with the camera, where the Barths kept it. You put the camera in your pocket and carried the recorder in its case. You went down the hall toward the living room and the fire escape. You had to pass the room where the man was sleeping, only he wasn't sleeping anymore. He saw you and you saw him. He didn't see the recorder because it was hidden at your side, behind your body. But he saw your face, your hair, your clothes. Even though you got away, he described you.

'You watched the papers. You knew you'd done it now, knew you'd put your ass in the chair. You didn't dare hock the stuff. You hid it away in the basement of the house where you lived with your brother. Meanwhile, you got a job in a wholesale grocery store and fed your habit that way and pulled a few heists . . .'

'I never said that.'

The thumb dug into the boy's chin. '*I* say that. You haven't kicked the habit, have you? You still need your jolt or two a day, don't you? So you heisted whenever you could. And watched the papers. And when you figured things had cooled off, you started thinking of hocking the ring, the camera, the recorder. But you were still afraid.

'Then you lost your job and needed money and met the old man, Abel Warner, in a bar. You'd met him before, maybe a year ago, when he was pushing a little H. He was small time and his H was full of cornstarch, but he'd been around a long time and knew fences all over New York. You got to talking and soon you asked him to pass the stuff for a cut. You gave him the ring and the camera and he went out to Long Island City. Everything seemed to go off okay, so you gave him the recorder. We were waiting and nailed Abel. You knew something had happened because he didn't show up at the bar and he wasn't at home. You started to sweat. You knew Mr Barth could identify you. You tried to stop him. You sent him a letter and made a few calls.'

D'Andrea paused to glance at Ted. 'You should've told

127

me, Mr Barth. I was almost too late putting that tail on you.'

'That was lucky for Bresk,' Ted said. 'Unlucky for me.'

D'Andrea turned back to the boy. 'You dyed your hair red. You started wearing that raincoat and hat. You were going out of your mind and tried to kill Barth. We got you. The end.' He leaned back. 'You want to add anything to that?'

The boy looked up. 'I want to take something away. Everything's right, the way it happened, except the killings. I swear I never killed those people. I found the ring in a tray on the dresser and she never woke up. I went to the kid's room and opened the closet and got the camera and the recorder and the kid never woke up. I went down the hall and the man was sitting up and he saw me and I ran to the window and made it to the street. The next day I read about the woman and the kid being killed.' He looked around. He saw several pairs of eyes move past him. He turned in his chair and looked at Ted. He half-rose. 'I swear, Mr Barth. May I burn in hell for all time. So help me, I never touched your wife and kid.'

'Then who did?' Ted said, voice hoarse. 'If not you, who?'

Bresk's lips moved and he dropped back into his chair and looked at D'Andrea. 'I don't know. Not me. I swear. Not me.'

'It was you,' D'Andrea said. 'Your prints match. Prints all over the window and one good one on the kid's dresser and a piece of thumb on the woman's doorknob. It was either you or Mr Barth. Now turn around and tell Mr Barth to his face that he killed his wife and his daughter.'

The boy slumped even lower. 'I swear,' he muttered, but all strength was gone from him now.

D'Andrea stood up. 'Take him out. Put him in Abel's cell. Maybe he'll save us the trouble of a trial like Abel did.'

The patrolman and the detective in brown went to Bresk and raised him up. The boy said, 'Abel's dead? Abel killed himself?'

'With a shirt,' D'Andrea said. 'Stuffed it down his throat. You got a shirt.'

The officers began to lead Bresk away. He pulled against

128

their arms, shook his head and shouted, 'The same cell? You mean you want me ... listen, bring a priest and I'll swear ... listen to me!'

'I'll listen to you when you're ready to sign a confession. Don't wait too long. That red hair of yours'll turn gray after twenty-four hours of cold turkey.'

The boy struggled and raised his legs and put back his head and howled like a dog. Ted shrank from the door as they carried him out. 'Ten, twelve hours,' Matt Oden said to D'Andrea.

The stenographer said, 'I doubt he'll last that long. He's almost in withdrawals now, and he's a punk kid. It's three forty-five. By eight, I figure.'

D'Andrea said, 'Just don't make a pool. That's all the newspapers have to hear.'

'Talking about newspapers,' Oden said, 'that guy from the *Daily News* is sniffing hard. We'd better let him in on it and ask for an off-the-record until we're ready. We'll have to book the kid by morning anyway.'

D'Andrea nodded. 'And call my buddy from the news service. He always spells my name right.'

Oden walked out and the stenographer followed. D'Andrea went to the two detectives near the window and spoke about checking Bresk's neighborhood as soon as it was light, and getting as much day-by-day information about the boy as possible. The two detectives left. Ted was alone with the lieutenant. 'Well, Mr Barth, it's over.'

'Is it?'

'The part that concerned you and me most is. Catching him. He's caught. And he's as good as convicted.'

'Is he?'

D'Andrea lit a cigarette and went to his chair and sat down and stretched out his legs. 'He is. This business is nothing. My own opinion is he'll crack in an hour or two. Carl – the stenographer – is right. Bresk's in the early stages of withdrawal right now. He was flat broke – had about twelve cents in his pockets. He probably hasn't had a fix in two, three days. I'll bet one of the reasons he attacked you was to get your dough. Two birds with one stone.'

'And when he confesses, that means he enters a plea of

129

guilty. Which in turn means he gets some sort of consideration, doesn't it?'

'He can't plead guilty to first-degree murder. And the D.A. won't let him cop a lesser plea. We've got a perfect case. You'll point him out in a court . . .'

Ted's eyes widened. 'We made a terrible mistake. I saw Bresk *before* picking him out of a lineup. His lawyer . . .'

D'Andrea sighed. 'His lawyer won't be Perry Mason, and this won't be a TV show with all sorts of surprises. It'll go nice and smooth. Bresk attacked you on the street. You saw him, fought him, almost killed him from what Matt tells me. So what's the point of a lineup?'

Ted moved to Bresk's chair and sat down facing the lieutenant. 'Well, I was just . . .'

'I know. You're trying to find ways Bresk can squirm out of the rap. But honestly, I can't see him getting off with anything less than life. And I know the D.A. will try for the chair. I *know*, Mr Barth, because I've talked it over with him.'

'How many go to the chair? What percentage, I mean?'

D'Andrea shrugged and flicked ashes from his cigarette.

'Not a very large percentage, I'll bet.'

'No, not any more.'

'And they'll bring in the poverty, the sickness of narcotics addiction, the youth of the poor orphan. He is an orphan, isn't he? He lives with his brother and his parents are dead?'

'Father abandoned the mother and three children. Mother died of TB four years ago.'

'That's even better. Abandoned child. Loveless. Strikes out at the world. Have mercy.' He stood up. 'He'll never burn.'

'Now you're making up TV shows again. He has a chance to burn and he has a chance to get life.'

'And life means parole some day. And my wife and daughter will never be paroled from their cells in the ground.'

'Let's wait until the trial before we begin to worry, shall we?'

Ted began to answer, and a phone rang. D'Andrea went to the window and grabbed the phone that was on the ledge. 'Yeah?' he said. And then, 'The mobile lab was here a few minutes ago. Maybe they're still here. Call the desk ... Yeah. I'll come down in about an hour ... No, I've been on late tour the past few months ... Yeah. Just finished the Barth case. A clean catch ... Thanks. See you.' He hung up..

Ted said, 'And now for bigger and better things. Life must go on. Weep we may but live we must.'

'That's right,' D'Andrea said, looking at him. His look was hard and unsympathetic. 'You once told me to find the killer. Then you'd go back to living like a human being, you said. Well, we found him. Now go back to living like a human being.'

'You found him, but that doesn't mean he'll ...'

'Or didn't you want us to find him?' D'Andrea interrupted, lips curling. 'Did you want to hang on to your excuse for bumming around and trying to get killed and refusing to face life?'

'Ah, Ted faces life, by Detective Lieutenant John D'Andrea. We're back to the soap opera.'

D'Andrea stood up. His anger was plain now. 'Yeah, we're back to the soap opera. We're back to saying you got no guts to live and it makes no difference that your reason was a good one. *Was*, mister, because you've survived nine months and it's all over and you either got to live or die now, not walk around half-way between. And I'll tell you something else. I don't give a damn. I'm tired of this particular soap opera. The ending's here. If the story drags on with a lot of crap about not being sure exactly what's going to happen to the killer, I'm tuning it out. It bores me.' He went to the door.

Ted said, 'You're right.'

D'Andrea turned.

'I *do* have to make up my mind whether to live or die. Though it's not really accurate to say "make up my mind". Make my mind obey my wish to live, everyone's wish to live, is closer to the truth. And you can help me. Just one more time.'

'Let you speak to the boy?'

'Alone.'

'Not alone. Never alone. And from *outside* his cell.'

'From outside his cell, but alone. He won't talk to me, really talk to me, if an officer is present.'

131

'The officer will be at the end of the hall, a good thirty-five feet away.'

'Then you'll let me?'

D'Andrea hesitated. 'Just what do you expect to gain?'

'I'm not sure. But something that will end the guilt. My guilt. My own self-torturing thoughts. If he'll confess to me, and it doesn't have to be in words – by a look, a nod of the head, any way at all. If he'll just end *my* part in their deaths . . .'

'Your part is all in your head. Your part can't be ended by the boy. If it could, it would have ended the minute he attacked you. He killed them. You know it and we know it and soon a judge and a jury will know it. Soon the whole city will know it. But what's in your head . . .' He shrugged.

'Maybe not ended. But *eased*. If I can just ease the guilt by making him admit . . .'

'It's crap. I don't believe it can help you, but okay.'

Ted mumbled his thanks and followed the lieutenant out to the hall and toward the staircase leading to the cells. His earlier feeling of light-headedness was back. He walked with the sensation of not quite touching the ground. Sound was soft, far away. Doors opened and shut in slow motion. He went down the metal staircase as if wrapped in cotton, D'Andrea floating along before him.

But through the haze of unreality, one thing remained real.

The lieutenant was right. Talking to Bresk wouldn't help. It wasn't talk he was going to give the boy.

It was death.

CHAPTER SEVENTEEN

He was alone with the boy. A uniformed policeman was at the far end of the concrete corridor, beyond the third cell, sitting on a chair and reading a newspaper. D'Andrea had spoken to the guard and walked back and looked in at Bresk and left. The boy was in the first cell. He sat on his cot – the same cot that Abel Warner had sat on – and watched Ted.

Ted moved up to the bars. 'It's time you and I had a talk.' He spoke softly so the guard wouldn't hear. He looked directly at Bresk and felt the unreality dissolving. Pain dissolved unreality, and it hurt to look at Bresk.

The boy stood up. He was pale and looked even paler with his unnaturally red hair. His eyes were rimmed in black. His hands trembled as he raised a cigarette to his mouth. 'Sure. Talk.'

'No one can hear us. I only want the truth. Just for my own peace of mind. For no other reason. We're alone here. Tell me. Nod your head. You killed them, didn't you?'

'No.' The mouth twitched. The face seemed about to dissolve. 'No, Christ, no.'

'Tell me, and I'll see that you get a doctor. I'll go across the way and get the doctor who treated me for a cut on my shoulder. I'll see he gives you a shot. It'll help you.'

'No! I want my brother.' The face was blinking and jerking and twitching. 'I want someone . . . a lawyer.'

'Tell me, and I'll phone your brother. Once he knows where you are, you'll get a lawyer. Once he knows where you are, the police can't stop you from having a lawyer. Tell me, and you'll get a doctor and a lawyer. Just nod. Even if the cell is bugged, a nod can't be recorded.'

'No,' the boy whispered. 'I won't. You can't make me. I'll die first.'

'Do you want to die?'

'I'd as soon.' He put his free hand into his pocket and came out with a crumpled pack of cigarettes and searched it and threw it away. He raised the small butt to his lips and dragged it and dragged it and had to drop it when it burned his fingers. He looked down at it and then at Ted. 'You got cigarettes?'

Ted shook his head.

'Hey, guard, I want a pack of cigarettes!'

Ted glanced down the hall. The guard didn't raise his eyes from his paper. He said, 'Nothing until breakfast. And then just food and coffee.'

'Oh, Christ,' the boy whispered. 'They're killing me.'

'Tell me,' Ted said. 'I'll go out and get you a carton of cigarettes. You killed them, didn't you? Nod. Whisper yes. Cigarettes and a doctor and your brother.'

The boy stared at him, lips moving soundlessly.

Ted took out his pack of cigarettes. 'I lied. Here. Just nod and you can have them.'

The boy moved his lips. Ted held the pack through the bars. The boy inched closer, leaned forward, raised his hand. Ted withdrew the pack. 'You can't grab it. I have to give it. Tell me. You killed them, didn't you?'

'No,' the boy said, his voice a rustling of dry grass, of dead leaves, of old paper on sidewalk. 'You know I didn't.'

'*I* know? Why not the lieutenant and the detectives and the stenographer? What do I know that they don't?'

'You were there,' the boy said, his eyes on the cigarettes. 'You have to know.'

'Well, maybe I do,' Ted said, and rested the hand with the cigarettes on the cell door's heavy crossbar. 'But I'm not sure. I thought you'd tell me ...' He rambled on, and the boy shuffled closer, and he said, 'When you left I ran out of the apartment, chasing you, not knowing you went out the window, and I was gone awhile. Maybe someone came in then and did it. Maybe an enemy ...' The boy was within arm's reach now; his eyes had left the cigarettes and were on Ted's face. 'Ten, fifteen minutes,' Ted said. 'Long enough ...'

'Did you tell that to the cops?' the boy said, and he came right up to the bars and his eyes were wide with hope and his voice was alive again. 'Did you tell that to the detective, the one ... D'Andrea? You gotta tell him. That's gotta be it. I know if you ...'

Ted had been figuring, planning, rejecting plans as Bresk drew closer and closer. Without the bars between them, there were a dozen swift ways of killing the boy – a dozen ways of chopping, choking and jabbing out his life before the guard could interfere. But with the bars, it was something else again. With the bars, he could only hope to pin him in place and work on his throat with one hand. And the guard might stop him before death came. But it was the only way.

The boy was saying, '... right now, Mr Barth. Please. Tell him and you'll see I never ...'

Ted's left arm shot in and curled around Bresk's neck. His right leg hit the bars and went through and hooked around the boy's left leg. His right hand closed on Bresk's throat, thumb pressing the voice box, paralyzing it.

Bresk never made a sound, but Ted was grabbed from behind, a thick arm hooking his neck, dragging him backward. There was a sharp pain in his left side and he groaned and let go. He was thrown back and hit the wall and slid into a sitting position, his left kidney agonized. He bit his lip and bent his head until the pain subsided. Then he looked up. D'Andrea was standing over him. The guard was asking Bresk if he was all right.

Bresk nodded and rubbed his throat and said, 'Listen, he said he ran out of the apartment and his wife and kid were alone for ten, maybe fifteen minutes and someone else, an enemy he said, someone else could've killed them. Ask him.'

Ted got up and brushed at his clothes. 'If I'd had a knife, it would all be over now. I just couldn't do it fast enough with my hands.'

'I was right outside that door,' D'Andrea said. 'I don't think you'd have made it even with a knife.'

'But ask him,' the boy shouted. 'Ask him about that ten minutes, will you?'

D'Andrea turned to the cell. 'Bresk, nothing on earth's going to save you.' He turned back to Ted. 'And nothing's going to stop him from reaching a courtroom.'

'But he said ...' the boy began.

D'Andrea sighed. 'He was getting you within reach. He knows you're guilty. I know you're guilty. You know you're guilty. Now go back to your cot and lie down. You haven't got much time to rest. You're going to be begging for death soon.'

135

The boy shook his head. He looked at Ted and D'Andrea and the guard. He moved his lips. He said, 'Isn't there any way . . .'

'No,' D'Andrea said. 'No way at all.' He told the guard to move his chair to Bresk's cell. He took Ted's arm and led him to the stairs and up them. He walked him along the hall, his grip tight, his voice even tighter. 'I could book you for that.'

Ted said nothing. They entered the desk room and went to the street door. D'Andrea released his arm. 'Stay away from here.'

Ted hesitated. D'Andrea opened the door and gave him a push. 'I mean it, Barth. You're on your own. No more cops and robbers. The D.A. will be in touch with you for certain legal matters and there'll be the trial. But that's it. I'm leaving orders you're to be kicked out if you stick your nose in here again.'

Ted started down the steps. The door slammed behind him. It was finished. To quote the lieutenant, he had to face life.

Teddy Faces Life, and the organ swells in a rich medley of sentimental old favorites. We find Teddy returning to his drab, dreary room, dreading an empty tomorrow.

Except that tomorrow, or later today, *wasn't* empty! Today was Sunday, and Sunday was his date with Susan.

It was now three thirty. In six or seven hours he would be driving out to the shore with her. And even though he hadn't eliminated Arthur, he could score points, could set himself up so that when he *did* eliminate Arthur she would fall to him easily, gladly, with love. There was even a chance (not just a chance, he told himself, but a *good* chance) that he wouldn't have to eliminate Arthur – that she would see how much he cared, how much he could do for her, how devoted he would be to her.

A man who had suffered as he had suffered deserved love. She would see that. She would respond to that.

He caught a cab. He lit a cigarette and crossed his legs and never looked back at Central Homicide.

By the time he reached the apartment, he had changed some of his thinking. Not that he wasn't still hopeful, but he had made a plan. As with an opponent in judo or on the streets, he bolstered hope with what was most likely to get results. In Susan's case, the cool, humorous, assured approach got results. He had never played that for what it was worth. He would do that today. At the same time, he would reach out for love, would offer love. Success depended on balancing the mixture correctly, just as the correct mixture of *nage-no-kata* and *katame-no-kata* was unbeatable in combat.

He smiled at his analogy, paid the cabby and entered the apartment. The correct mixture of throws and groundwork: an exact analogy when dealing with a woman.

He undressed immediately. He wanted to be rested and fresh for combat. And to play it safe he took another of his sleeping pills.

CHAPTER EIGHTEEN

His clock was set for ten, but he was torn from heavy slumber at eight thirty. He stumbled to the phone and picked it up and cleared his throat. 'Yes?'

'Mr Barth, this is Matt Oden at Central Homicide. Lieutenant D'Andrea asked me to call you. Bresk confessed an hour ago. He signed the statement and said he used the same knife he used on you. He's arraigned and it's all wrapped up.'

Ted absorbed that in silence.

'Well, see you in court. 'Course, that won't be for some time yet.'

'Yes. Thank you.'

'Sure.' The line clicked.

Ted went back to bed.

The wind was hot and numbed his cheeks and dried his lips. Susan's hair blew in all directions – back and up and into her face – but she laughed and talked of her old sports car and how she missed it. He drove the rented convertible along the Belt Parkway toward Jones Beach, glancing at her every so often. She was big and beautiful and exciting in a short yellow shift. He complimented her on it.

'This thing?' She looked down at herself. 'It's just to cover the bathing suit I'm wearing.'

He said he was wearing his shorts. 'Red latex,' he said, and winked. 'Real sexy.'

'Crazy. We're a team. I've taken a chance today. Lost two pounds so I'm wearing the bikini.'

He asked what color bikini and squinted into the haze of sunlight and exhaust fumes.

'Sunset Rose, the tag said.'

'Let's see.'

'You mean now, here?'

'Sure. Why not?'

She raised herself off the seat and drew the skirt all the way to her waist. Her thighs were longer than he had thought they would be – and leaner. Beautiful thighs. The fine-colored bikini bottom was thin and tight, outlining her pubic area in a plump V.

A shout and a whistle cut short his examination. He looked up to see a green sedan in the right-hand lane. It was keeping pace with them. The crew-cut boy behind the wheel was grinning; the boy beside him was almost in his lap, whistling and yelling.

'Enough there for all three of us!' the passenger yelled.

Susan yanked down her skirt.

'Aw, honey,' the driver protested, 'that's square.'

Ted floored the gas pedal and the new convertible shot ahead. He was raging, but Susan laughed and said, 'Anyway, that's Sunset Rose.'

'I didn't notice,' Ted said, making himself smile, reminding himself that today he was loose and easy and humorous; today he was playing Susan's game. 'It was that birthday-skin white that got me.'

She laughed again and took cigarettes from her bag. He pressed the lighter for her. He heard a whistle. The green sedan was back on the right. Susan said, 'Go away, little men,' and lit her cigarette.

'You sure we all can't share the wealth?' the driver shouted.

Susan turned her back on them. 'What do you think of surf bathing as compared with swimming in a pool?'

Ted answered conversationally, but his neck was tight and his face burned from more than the wind. He tried to pull away, but the green sedan kept pace.

He didn't plan on it. He thought he would ignore the kids until they went away. But there was laughter from the green sedan and he suddenly couldn't stand it. He roared ahead, cut hard right and heard a scream of brakes.

'Lord,' Susan murmured and looked back.

He continued in the right lane. 'Just a little discipline.'

'Let's turn off at the next exit and lose them. Then we'll get back on the parkway ...'

He said, 'That's not necessary,' and thought that Susan had never seen him fight. He wondered if she would be impressed with his skill or whether it would upset her.

The green sedan came up on his left. The boy on the

passenger's side was no longer laughing. He shouted, 'You wanna play, we'll play.' The green sedan cut in toward him.

Ted didn't give an inch. He looked at the green sedan and smiled. Susan said, 'They'll hit us, Ted!' He said, 'So the rental company will replace a fender.' The green sedan swerved away at the last possible minute. It tried to pull ahead, but Ted knew they wanted to duplicate his cut-off maneuver so he kept the convertible a few feet out front. They were doing eighty when he came up behind a black hardtop and had to slow. The green sedan also slowed, waiting for him.

Once again Ted didn't plan it. Once again the redness swept him and he reacted to it. The green sedan was close alongside and the boy on the passenger's side put his head out to say something and Ted leaned out and said, 'I'm going to kill both of you.' He said it loud enough for the boy to hear and soft enough to hope Susan wouldn't. He slowed even more, and the boy stared at him, and he said, 'Pull onto the grass and we'll settle this.' The green sedan dropped back and cut in behind him and he pulled the convertible onto the grass and bumped along to a stop.

'Ted, there are two of them,' Susan said, face pale.

'Watch carefully,' he said, and opened the door and got out. The green sedan hadn't come up onto the grass. It was crawling by on the parkway, as if to mount the grass in front of the convertible. The two boys were talking to each other and gesticulating excitedly. Then the passenger stuck his head out the window and shouted an obscenity. Ted laughed. The green sedan shot away in a burst of blue exhaust and a scream of tortured rubber.

Ted went back to the convertible. 'They'll drive like maniacs,' he said, 'but they won't be able to outrace the truth. That they're chicken.'

'I can understand *why* they were chicken.'

'Two of them to my one?'

'Your one was a bad-looking one. I think you really meant that about killing them.'

'Don't be silly.' He started the car.

'No more trouble today, Ted. Save your antagonism for girls who enjoy brawls.'

Her sharpness of voice upset him. 'You act as if I started it.'

'They were flirting. If you'd ignored them, they'd have gone away. Haven't you ever flirted with a woman when she was with another man?'

'Not like that.'

'Think back to when you were a boy. How else does a boy flirt?'

He was watching for a break in traffic, but turned and looked at her. 'I'm too old to remember.'

'Now your antagonism is turning on *me*. Now you want to fight with *me*.'

'There was a definite implication . . .'

'I can spend my Sundays in more productive ways than this. Would you like to return to the city?'

He didn't answer. He drove onto the parkway and put on the radio. Rock-'n-roll music came on. He began to change the station, then glanced at her.

'I'm young,' she said, 'but not common.'

He found WQXR. After a few moments of music, she said, 'Hector Berlioz.'

He smiled at her. She returned his smile. He reached over and put his hand on her thigh and squeezed it. She raised her eyebrows but didn't stop him. 'Sit closer,' he said. She slid across the seat. 'Closer. Right up against me,' She complied.

He kept his hand on her leg and felt her body against his and inhaled her fragrance. Later, traffic piled up and he was able to turn from the road and touch her face with his lips. 'Susan,' he said, fighting to keep his voice even.

'Watch where you're driving.'

His fingers stroked her thigh through the yellow cotton dress. His heart pounded and his mouth grew dry with desire. Traffic began to move. 'You know what I'd like to do?' he said.

'Give me three guesses.'

'Skip Jones Beach and keep driving . . . about two hours more to a little bay area I know. There's a pebbled beach and a seafood stand and a dock and boats to rent.'

'But why bother? I've got a basket full of food and two thermoses . . .'

'And a little motel behind the dunes.' His hand tightened

141

on her leg. 'We could drive back early tomorrow morning.'

She pulled away. She slid clear across the seat to the door. 'Spare me your fantasies.'

He tried to keep it light. 'You can't blame a guy for trying, can you?'

'I can, if the guy never received any encouragement.'

Again he reacted without planning. Again he was carried away by a rush of feeling, and whispered, 'It's not just ... Susan, you must know how I feel.' He was afraid to look at her.

She was quiet for what seemed to be a long time; then she said, 'I guess I do. I didn't want to admit it, but I do. I like you very much, Ted. And after ... what happened to you, I wanted to help. But I've never considered ...'

'Let's not go into that now. I made a mistake. It's much too early in the game to go into that.'

'It'll never get later.'

Now he had to look at her, his heart sinking; the urge to weep and beg and reach out and take moved over him. He fought it back and smiled. 'We never really know, do we?' And before she could answer, said, 'Here comes our exit.'

It was all going wrong. From the beginning it had gone wrong, and now, as he lay in the sun beside the beautiful blonde girl, it was getting worse. Desire had been growing, along with despair. Self-control had been shrinking, along with hope.

They had been in the water. He had taken her in his arms as a large wave had hit, and kissed her and run his hands over her body. She had shoved him away angrily and swum far out, and he had returned to the gray beach blanket, finally unable to deny that she cared nothing for him.

Later, as she lay face down, eyes closed, he had put his mouth to her ear and whispered, 'Susan, give me a chance. I want to marry you.'

She hadn't stirred.

Now it was four thirty and she roused herself and said, 'I must have dozed,' and didn't look at him. She got a sandwich from the wicker basket and asked if he wanted one.

'No. I'd like a drink.'

She reached for the thermos.

'Not fruit juice. A distillation thereof.'

142

She unwrapped her sandwich. 'I'll make you a martini when we get to my place.'

He searched her face, desperate for some sign of warmth, of affection – some sign on which to build hope for the future. Because he couldn't seem to visualize a future without Susan. And this had been true for a long time, longer than he had consciously known.

She finally met his eyes. She reached out and took his hand. 'I'm sorry. I just can't feel that way about you. And I'm not very good at playing along. Perhaps if I hadn't met Arthur ...'

'All right,' he said harshly, and got up and went across the hot sand, past the talking, laughing, happy people, to the ocean. He entered the water and it was cold, but not as cold as the chill that had settled over him a moment ago.

He threw himself into a wave and began to swim; and he was swimming in a sea of hopelessness. He stroked harder, faster, and was far out and alone; and he thought how easy it would be to keep going until strength failed and the cold immensity closed over him and the blackness came and it was finished.

And he thought of the plump V of Susan's pubic area and the swelling whiteness of her breasts and the long whiteness of her thighs and the bursting whiteness of her buttocks. That Susan – the Susan of flesh ... the Susan of viable sexual responses and moist tubes – that Susan was attainable if the one behind the pale blue eyes wasn't.

He turned back toward shore. When he came to the blanket he bent for a towel and grinned and said, 'That was what I needed ... a long swim to work off the blues.'

She nodded solemnly.

He dropped down beside her, toweling his hair, and said, 'C'mon now. Let's enjoy this day, no matter what we did or said before. It's boy and girl and sunshine and ... that reminds me of a joke.'

He told her the joke, and she burst into laughter and said, 'Whoo, that's sick!' and laughed some more and then told him one.

CHAPTER NINETEEN

He kept it light and funny all the way back to Manhattan. He kept Susan smiling and laughing and responding as they drove along the parkway and through the city. It was seven thirty when they stopped in front of her apartment, and he said, 'Why yes, thank you, Susan. *I would* like to come in for a moment.'

She glanced away from him. 'I don't know, Ted. I'm tired and I feel so tacky in this damp bathing suit.'

'I wanted to take a locker, didn't I?' (Smile, smile, smile.)

'Yes, but I figured it was such a short ride home . . .'

'That martini, remember?' He got out of the car and walked around to the street side and opened the door. His skin felt tight and hot, and he wondered whether it was sunburn or the blood pounding up inside him.

'All right. Just one.'

They went down the steps to the door beside the stoop. She bent to the lock and her yellow shift clung to her damp bathing suit and his hands rose as if to press the round swellings. She opened the door and he followed her inside. He felt strange and uncomfortable. He had been here twice before, but never with such thoughts. 'Where's Hank?'

'Didn't I tell you? In Tarrytown with the family. He won't be back until late.'

He said, 'Oh, yes, I'd forgotten,' but he hadn't. He had just wanted to hear it again – wanted to make absolutely sure so that his plan would grow stronger. This time he wouldn't react rashly. This time he would knew exactly what he was doing. And afterwards she would understand what he felt, what he could give her.

The apartment had a long, narrow living room funneling into a gloomy little foyer which passed a compact kitchen. It ended in a bedroom, with a bathroom attached. Susan slept in the bedroom, Hank on the convertible couch in the living room.

'I just have to get out of this suit, Ted. Aren't you uncomfortable in yours?'

He said he was, and that he would slip out of it while she was changing.

'I'm going to shower too. You can use the bedroom while I'm in the bathroom.'

He said fine and he would have a martini ready for her when she came out. 'The makings still in the kitchen cabinet?'

'Yes.' She turned to the foyer. 'Oh, the basket. I left it in the car. Would you bring it in?'

He went outside. The street was quiet; the day faded toward darkness. He paused a moment, thinking he could get in the car and drive away and never come back. He could drive to California where it was Spring all year long ... where he knew no one and no one knew him ... where he could live on the stock and his savings and meet new people, new women ... where he could live a new life. He was free of the boy and he was free of Laura and Wallace and he could be free of Susan.

Then he thought of her body in the tight bikini, and he went back to the apartment and put the basket on the floor beside the couch. He heard a door close. He moved softly to the foyer and the kitchen and found the gin and vermouth. He didn't bother to mix martinis. He poured gin into a glass and drank it down and stood listening.

Water began to run in the bathroom. He went to the bedroom. He took off his shoes and stockings and then his shirt and then his trousers. He pulled off the damp bathing trunks and let them drop to the floor, and looked at his clothes lying on the bed. There was still time to be free of Susan.

He heard her voice. She was singing in the shower. He moved around the bed to the window near the bathroom door and drew the shade.

He tried the door. It was locked. He put his shoulder to it and pressed, still trying to be gentle, still trying to be quiet. But this wasn't anything gentle and quiet, and he stepped back and drew himself together and lunged forward with all his weight and all his strength. The door opened with a sharp, splintering sound, the simple tongue mechanism tearing free. Directly in front of him, horizontal to the door, was the bath-tub, its curtain drawn, water hissing from the shower neck on the right wall. Behind it, Susan's voice stopped singing ... and he tensed for what would follow. Then she called, 'I'm in the shower, Ted,' and he realized she thought he had knocked.

He closed the door quietly. She began singing again, and he moved toward the rustling plastic curtain and saw movement behind it and felt excitement stir low in his body. He came right up to the curtain and stopped. He touched the plastic with his fingertips and thought how her naked body was only inches away from his naked body – and his excitement grew.

He tore open the curtain and she was facing the nozzle, head up and body streaming water. She looked at him, mouth opening, and he stepped over the side of the tub and jerked the curtain back into place as he had closed the door, shutting himself away with Susan.

She surprised him. She didn't scream. She didn't strike out at him. She tried to back away, but there was no place to back. He pinned her arms to her sides by putting both of his around her. He pressed her to the wall, telling her how beautiful she was with her heavy conical breasts and rounded belly and thick thatch of hair and long, strong legs. Harsh breathing was her only answer.

The water was warm. It ran from his hair and face and body and was a soft sound in his ears. It soothed him and he bent and kissed her shoulder and neck, and raised his head and kissed her lips. She was absolutely rigid. He said, 'Susan, listen to me, I love you,' and took his right arm from around her, wanting to remove the white bathing cap, wanting to see her hair fall free.

She raked his face with her left hand, the nails gouging his cheeks, making him cry out. She said, 'Dirty, dirty bastard,' and tried to rake again, but he punched her in the temple and she fell sideways. He stopped her from going down and tore off her cap. Her head sagged forward against his chest, the blond hair going dark under the soaking stream. He put both hands on her bottom, cupping the large wet cheeks, grinding himself into her. She bit his chest, piercing the flesh of his right breast. Again he cried out, and again he struck her – a chop at the back of the neck this time. Her jaw sagged open and she began to slide down. He held her upright, shoved back her head, saw she was near unconsciousness.

146

He didn't want her to be unconscious. He kept her standing until her eyes cleared; then he said, 'Don't fight me, Susan. It's no use. Let me love you, Susan.' His lips went back to her lips and his hands to her bottom. He inserted a finger between the cheeks, and when she didn't fight him he bent his knees, lowering himself until he could kiss her breasts. He took the left one in his mouth and felt the nipple rise in mammary erection.

Now she would love him. Now the pain they had exchanged would add to the fury of their mating. Now he would train her to passion she would never be able to duplicate and never be able to forget.

Still kissing her breast, he put one hand on her belly, moving it down to the springy hair, down to the center of Susan and the center of Ted and the joining of Susan and Ted.

She tried to knee him in the groin. He was open and there was only one defense. He fell backward – fell through the curtain and out of the tub and onto the cold tile floor. He tucked in his chin and used his arms to break the fall, and reached up as she tried to run over him to the door. He grabbed a leg and a wrist and pulled her down on top of him. She shrieked, 'Help!' three times before he rolled her onto her back and chopped her under the nose and felt her go limp.

He got to his knees. She lay with her head on the side. A trickle of blood ran from her nose to the floor.

The blood bothered him. He went to a towel rack and came back and wiped her clean. She began to roll her head and moan. He put the towel down and put himself between her legs and waited. She was beautiful and abundant, and he was filled with fire and wanted her as he had never wanted any other woman. But he waited. He waited because she was going to be fully conscious when he took her. He waited because she was going to serve him with movement, with passion, simulated or otherwise.

She moved her legs. He stroked them with his left hand. When her eyes opened, he raised his right hand over her face and said, 'Susan, pay strict attention. We're going to make love now. You're going to help me. If not ...' He made a brief, chopping motion.

147

She stared at him. She put her hand to her nose and whispered, 'You must be crazy.'

He bent forward and began to caress her body. She moaned. He came all the way forward and kissed her lips. She jerked her head aside. He raised himself and gave her a stiff-fingered jab under the rib cage. She choked and convulsed, her legs drawing up, her mouth moving spasmodically. He covered her mouth in case she decided to scream. He used his other hand to stroke the underside of her thighs and buttocks, brought into prominence by the drawn-up legs.

When her legs came down, he took his hand from her mouth. 'We'll try again,' he said, keeping his voice cold. But he was burning inside – burning for the big white cheeks and the fat breasts – burning for the long, white body now covered with goose bumps.

He bent forward and kissed her. She trembled and stayed still. He raised himself and brought his hand before her eyes and said, 'I'm afraid that's not enough. You have to *give*, Susan. We'll try again.'

He bent forward and kissed her again. Her lips opened and her hand moved onto his back. She trembled violently, but that was all right. That was really quite good. The cool Miss Susan Shore trembled with fear of her master.

He put a hand beneath her buttocks and pinched and probed. She gasped and tried to raise herself away from his hand. He pressed down on her, and her thighs closed on him, as if to prevent him from entering; but he entered and she didn't fight and he raised his mouth and whispered, 'You've had some experience. Show it.'

Her eyes were squeezed shut and tears trickled from under the lids and she didn't respond; she just lay passive, trembling, weeping. He struck her on the side of the neck, hard enough to let her know that particular sense of agonized paralysis. She cried out and her legs went up and around him and her arms closed over his back and even though the tears came faster she moved and moved well.

He kissed her wet face and kneaded her buttocks and plowed her body and the fire was on him and he hurt her with his hands and smothered her cries with his lips and went on, went on . . .

148

CHAPTER TWENTY

He rested on her until she whimpered in his ear: 'Please, please, let me up. Please, Ted, please.'

He raised himself and stood over her. She looked up, mouth puffy and trembling, red splotches on the white expanse of her body. The tears still trickled down her cheeks. 'Can I sit up?' she whispered.

He nodded and helped her.

'Can I wash?'

'Yes, but stay in here.'

He went out of the bathroom, closing the door behind him. He took the bedspread off the bed and toweled himself and got into his clothes. He put his bathing suit on the chair, where he would see it and remember to take it with him. Then he opened the bathroom door. She was sitting on the closed toilet seat, wearing a pink, terrycloth bathrobe. She was bent over, hands clasped in her lap, but she jerked erect when she saw him. He said, 'Take off the robe and come in here.'

'You can't mean . . .'

He raised his right hand, fingers extended stiffly.

She jumped up, tearing off the robe, eyes fixed on his hand.

He went to the bed and sat down at the edge. She came out, hunched over like an old woman. 'Stand up straight,' he said.

She straightened and her breasts stuck out. He nodded. 'That's my beautiful Susan.'

'Please, Ted,' she whispered. 'No more now. Tomorrow, if you want, but I feel ill now. Please, Ted, let me rest. I won't make trouble for you. I swear I won't.'

'I know you won't,' he said, and patted his knee. 'Come here.'

She came to him and sat down and he put an arm around her waist, cupping one breast, and stroked her thighs with the other hand. Her body still trembled. He smiled. He kissed her shoulder and rubbed her breast and his smile widened. She had been good. The best yet. But he was free of her now. He had thought he would become thoroughly chained, but it hadn't worked out that way. He was free of Susan, and all that remained was to see he stayed free of the law.

'I'm not coming back tomorrow,' he said. 'I'm never coming back again.'

Her trembling lessened.

'I know you're relieved. You can admit it.'

She glanced at him once, quickly, and then away. 'I . . . after something like this . . . but I know you lost your head . . .'

He laughed. He rubbed her nipple and she said, 'Don't, please,' and he laughed again.

'I'm off the hook with you, Susan. I've had you and you're wonderful but it's different now. I was lucky. I'm going to leave the city. You'll never see me again. That really tears you apart, doesn't it?'

She seemed about to speak and he pinched her breast and she grunted and said nothing. Again he laughed, and then he stopped laughing. 'Now we come to the last order of business. The most important order of business. Your forgetting that this ever happened.'

'Forgetting . . . you mean . . . I said I wouldn't make trouble.'

'So you did. But I'd like to be sure. That's why I want you to know I've seen Arthur.'

'You've seen . . .'

'Twice. Wednesday night and Saturday night. Or more exactly, Thursday morning and Sunday morning, after you returned from your dates. I followed him both times. I was going to break him up a little, but both times something interfered. Now I no longer want to hurt him.'

Her eyes were fixed on his. She sat on his lap, nude, and her trembling increased and her mouth moved and she said nothing.

'But if you try any foolishness, if you contact the police and make any wild accusations . . . rape or any such nonsense, I promise you he'll spend months in the hospital.'

'I . . . I won't, Ted.'

He believed her. She was thoroughly cowed. He smiled

and patted her rump and said, 'Not that you could make it stick. But the little lesson you just learned is only a kindergarten course in pain. What I could do to a boy like Arthur . . .' He smiled. 'He wouldn't even *be* a boy after that.'

She nodded intently. 'It's forgotten. I swear, Ted. How could I go to the police anyway? Rape is so subjective. Who could judge where your will ended and mine began? You probably know I began to enjoy it somewhere along the way, don't you? Even pain is sexual . . .'

She went on, verbalizing her terror, and he felt one small pang because so much of that terror was for Arthur.

He told her to get up and she obeyed like a frightened child. He said he was leaving and she nodded. 'I'll see you to the door.' He laughed and said she needn't bother.

She stood waiting for instructions as he went to the chair and picked up his bathing trunks. He said, 'Go on, get dressed,' and walked down the foyer and through the living room. He opened the door – and froze.

Lieutenant D'Andrea and Matt Oden were standing there, talking. They looked at him, and D'Andrea said, 'Some last few details . . .' Ted heard Susan weeping and the sound grew wilder and he saw that Oden, who stood closest to him, had also heard it. And how had they known he was here unless they had followed him? And why had they followed him?

Susan's voice rose in hysteria and Oden said, 'What's going on?' and D'Andrea said, 'What is it, Matt?' Ted tried to step back, but Oden came bulling in with his big body and Ted didn't have room to breathe and didn't have time to think. He turned and ran inside, going just far enough to free his arm of the door. As Oden came after him. Ted dropped his bathing trunks and swung a full, right stroke, palm down and chopping edge out, and caught Oden in the larynx. The big man toppled without a sound. Ted felt sure he was dead because it had been an unobstructed, full-strength chop, the first he had ever delivered to anything other than a practice bag, and it seemed to have landed straight on.

D'Andrea said, 'Why . . .' and came rushing in, his hand digging back to where Ted was sure he kept his gun in a hip-pocket holster. Ted met him just past Oden's body, and gripped his wrists and used his knees. D'Andrea was strong, as strong as Ted had thought he was, and he blocked Ted's knees and shoved forward.

Ted still couldn't think. Everything had come crashing down and his brain whirled and he pushed against D'Andrea's weight, holding desperately to the man's hands, pressing them back past his waist, holding especially hard to the right hand that had drawn a snub-nosed little revolver from the back pocket and was trying to bring it past the hip, trying to bring it forward to bear on Ted.

He couldn't think, but he knew what he had done. He had raped Susan. He had killed Oden. And the detectives had come here for something else ... something else they had learned he had done ...

He managed to kick past D'Andrea and kick the door shut so that no one from outside could make the odds impossible. Behind him in the bedroom Susan still wept wildly, but she was no menace.

He was beginning to think a little. He set himself and shoved at D'Andrea with all his strength and waited until D'Andrea countered with all *his* strength, and suddenly gave way, collapsing and falling over backward, tucking his knees into his belly. D'Andrea couldn't hold back and fell on top of him. Ted dug his feet into the lieutenant's body and shoved up and D'Andrea went flying. Ted let go of his wrists. It was a chance he had to take.

As soon as D'Andrea was over him, he scrambled erect, twisting about. D'Andrea had landed near the couch. He was on his side, stunned, but the gun was still in his right hand. Ted threw himself forward, and D'Andrea's head turned. Ted was in midair and everything seemed to go into slow motion. D'Andrea's eyes widened and he raised his gun hand, but it was in the wrong position; it had to be turned around and pointed at Ted and there wasn't enough time for that. He threw the gun away from Ted, and Ted landed on him.

The lieutenant kneed him in the groin. Agony invested Ted's lower body and he screamed and chopped at the lieutenant's face. He managed to get over him and scramble around to the other side of the couch and rise, biting his lip and crouching over and waiting for the pain to ease so he could defend himself. He needed a minute. He desperately needed a minute of rest.

D'Andrea also got up, but his mouth was bleeding and he staggered, gasping for breath. 'You maniac.' Ted knew he had his minute. D'Andrea was no longer a young man. D'Andrea was hurt and played out. D'Andrea was using talk to mask his fear. 'Matt finally mentioned your following a man. I was worried you might've slipped your cable. I wanted to protect that man. I wanted to protect you.'

Ted sucked air. He stood between D'Andrea and the foyer. And the gun had landed in the foyer. And he could stop D'Andrea from reaching the door. In a while he would come around the couch and give the cop the worst beating of his life – the last beating of his life.

D'Andrea glanced at Oden, who was lying to the left of the door. 'We've got to get him to a doctor. You realize . . .'

Ted straightened a bit; the pain had begun to recede. He shuffled a half-step toward the end of the couch near the foyer. But it was a feint. In a moment he would hurdle the couch and kick D'Andrea's brains out. In a moment he would finish the lieutenant, get in the car and drive away, leaving all this madness behind.

D'Andrea jumped back and tore at his jacket and drew out a short, black tube. A blackjack. 'You maniac. Who else have you killed?'

Ted stopped. The blackjack changed things. One blow on the head and he would lose consciousness. He had to make sure he struck first, a long kick to the guts. Or a flying kick to the heart – a deadly *karate* kick he hadn't practiced too often and wasn't too sure of. But it might be the only way.

He moved another half-step toward the end of the couch, no longer feinting. He had to come around and get a clear shot at the heavyset officer.

D'Andrea backed a little and crouched a little. Even with a weapon, he was afraid. The big tough cop was afraid and Ted smiled and reached the end of the couch. He was going to enjoy this.

And then D'Andrea spoke and Ted's smile died and his face twisted. 'The kid said he found the ring on the dresser.

153

You said your wife always wore the ring. And right at the beginning, in November, when I took statements, there was one from your brother-in-law, Wallace Stegman. He said . . .'

Ted came around the couch fast. The lieutenant lunged forward, swinging down with the blackjack, his face white and his eyes staring. Ted wasn't set and had to leap back, but he landed in position.

The lieutenant wouldn't bite. He stood stiff, chest heaving. 'Stegman said his sister always took off her college ring. Before your marriage. When they lived at home . . .'

Ted took three short dancing steps. The lieutenant whipped the blackjack back and forth, back and forth, and glanced quickly behind him and backed up and said, 'Habits can change, but what if your wife's didn't? Why would you lie?'

Ted had stopped. His head hurt. There was a terrible tension in him. He had to kill this man – had to kill him before he said any more. He feinted a leap, and again the lieutenant didn't bite. D'Andrea swung his blackjack back and forth and seemed to be breathing more easily. And that blackjack had to be watched. That blackjack could end it with one lucky blow.

'Why would you lie, unless you wanted to frame the kid? If he took the ring from the dresser he might not have wakened your wife, might not have had to kill her. But if he tore it off her finger she had to be awake, or had to be dead, and it would follow that he had nothing to lose in killing the child. So you said he took it off her finger. Did you do it for the stock?'

Ted knew his next move. He stepped back, as if suddenly stunned, as if suddenly afraid. D'Andrea leaned forward, about to reverse direction, and that was what Ted was waiting for. Now he would scream his *keeyi* and launch himself feet first and the blackjack wouldn't reach his head. The lieutenant would fall with his chest crushed, and if he wasn't dead Ted would kick the life out of him.

'Could you kill your own daughter, Barth? Could you really . . .'

Ted's body coiled and he put his right foot back, as if to move farther away, and his knees bent and he was ready. And

154

the lieutenant bit at last, stepping forward, enthralled by his own words, and Ted said, 'Now!'

Movement caught the corner of his eye. Movement from where Oden lay. And as he tried to launch himself into the double kick, something struck him a terrible blow in the stomach and he fell backward. There was a roar of sound; and then he felt pain as he had never felt pain before. His belly was filled with molten metal.

He screamed, and as he did he thought of the movement he had caught from the corner of his eye. Oden hadn't died; Oden had shot him. And then he thought of another movement caught from the corner of his eye – another movement leading to disaster. And he screamed again – for agony nine months removed. And D'Andrea's words beat at his mind and a barrier, a protective stockade, fell in ruins and he spoke in a high, childish voice: 'Daddy, I saw you. Daddy, I saw you.'

He awoke quite suddenly and sat up and blinked his eyes in the darkness. For a moment he thought Myra had awakened him for work. Then he remembered he was in the guest room and she was in the bedroom, and besides it was too dark for morning, even a November morning.

He hadn't had a nightmare. He'd had plenty of them lately, but not tonight – not that he could remember. Certainly not the one in which he was fondling a girl and couldn't see her face but her voice was the blond trainee's and he called her by her name, Susan, and then realized it was Myra and she was old and obese and he couldn't let her go and she turned to putrefaction in his arms and it ran down his body and he too became putrefaction.

No, he would remember if it was that one.

He was tired. He had worked hard hours, long hours, since Monday morning. And he hadn't been sleeping well because of the nightmares and the confused thinking which preceded the nightmares.

He was about to lie down again when he heard it. Movement in the room next to his. Debbie's room. And then the movement passed to the hall and a floorboard squeaked and he looked at the open door. The boy came into sight and they looked at each other and the boy ran.

155

He jerked into motion, feet hitting the floor . . . and then stopped. He sat there, and everything fell into place and truth had him by the throat.

He hated working for Drizer Chemical, had hated every job he had ever had, hated the wasting of his life's sweet hours. He didn't really hate Myra – only what her presence did to his life. It kept him from freedom, from love and sunshine and a world of places to go. She saw her inheritance – a hundred seventy-five thousand dollars in blue-chip securities – as a trust for Debbie and for Wallace's children. He saw it as his life and he wanted to live it.

He stood up, his path crystal clear. He made sure the intruder had left and went to the kitchen and found Myra's rubber gloves in the sink. He pulled them on and took the small, sharp steak knife from the drawer and went back into the hall to Debbie's room. He closed the door softly, heard it click, waited to make sure his child still slept. Then he went to the master bedroom.

Myra's breathing was deep and regular. She and Debbie had slept right through the intruder's visit. But that wouldn't be the way the police would get it. The intruder had killed Myra when she had awakened, and had fled before Ted could stop him. Ted and Debbie would leave this place, would start a new life, perhaps with the lovely young trainee as part of it. They would travel all over the country, all over the world. He would waste no more precious hours in offices. He would waste no more inner strength in self-deception.

He closed the door and went to the bed. Myra lay on her side, mouth open, heavy and coarse and in his way. He had quarrelled with her as his father had quarrelled with his mother. He had hated life with her as his father had hated life with his mother. Now it would end.

He hesitated, marshalling all his arguments, all his courage. He hesitated, until she sighed and flung out an arm and seemed about to waken. Then he poised the knife just under her ear, sucked breath and slit her throat.

As he did, as she coughed and leaped up and fell back, he saw movement from the corner of his eye – he saw a blur of white and heard a tiny cry and turned his head. And he remembered that he hadn't heard the lock click on this door.

156

On Debbie's door, yes, but not on this door. This door had opened soundlessly. God! This door had opened on his act of murder.

Debbie was there in her white nightgown and white face and staring eyes. Debbie was there, and it shouldn't have been. God! It shouldn't have been. He had taken precautions. He had closed her door and closed this door and she shouldn't be here. Not this Debbie. Not such fear, such horror in her eyes. Not such fear, such horror of him.

No, it shouldn't have been – couldn't be. He turned from Myra, hearing the final, awful gurgle. He held the knife. He couldn't let it go, couldn't put it down anywhere because it had to be broken with the pliers and flushed down the toilet in little pieces along with the shredded gloves; he couldn't let it touch his clothing or anything else. He came toward her, smiling and nodding and waiting for words to explain away the fear and horror. (What words were there, God? What magic to wipe away the fear and horror?)

She backed from him. He said, his voice ringing in the hollow cavern that was his brain, 'Debbie, I found Mother ...'

She backed down the foyer to her room. She said, 'Daddy, I saw you,' and the fear and horror were impossible. He followed her into her room, talking, saying he had found Mother that way and had picked up the knife; and she said, 'Daddy, I saw you.'

He shook his head, the words drying up in him. (The magic, God, bring on the magic because it was impossible this way, impossible to live with the fear and horror in her eyes, God, impossible.)

She climbed into her bed and lay huddled there. She said, 'Daddy, I saw you. Daddy, I saw you.' And he knew he had to end her fear, had to end her horrer. And he bent to her and mumbled her name and did it as he had done it to Myra. And he used the pliers and he flushed the toilet and his mind slipped.

Ted Barth, as he had been, never left that bathroom. Ted Barth, as he became, woke up in the darkness and saw the boy and found his family butchered and began his search. Ted Barth forgot what he could not tolerate to remember.

But the forgetting was short of perfect, as he himself was short of being mad. Ted Barth danced on a tightrope above a pit of remembrance.

And now a bullet had toppled him into that pit. And he wasn't surprised at what he found there. The pit had always been waiting close beneath him. The pit had often tried to reach up and engulf him. He had wanted the boy's confession because of the pit. He had wanted the boy's death because of the pit. He'd had moments of wanting his own death because of the pit.

D'Andrea's face swung into view like a huge sun filling a darkening sky. Yet his voice was far away. 'You don't have to say any more. Lie quiet. I've called an ambulance.'

There was an awful hole in his body – his strong, trained, invisible body. Everything was leaking out of that hole. His life was leaking out of that hole.

He spoke, and he too was far away. 'I said things?'

'You said everything.' Far away voice. Far, far away and full of loathing.

Ted said, or thought he said, 'I never meant to hurt Debbie. I killed myself when I killed her. It was the same thing.' (Yet he feared dying, now that it was upon him. He feared dying and he feared anyone's knowing it and he didn't want to die. God, he didn't want to die.)

The lieutenant's face swam above him, grim and silent.

'You believe that, don't you?'

No answer.

'You must believe that!'

Still no answer. The face seemed to be receding. There was no sound in all the world other than a dim, faltering drum beat. And then that too was gone.

And then his pain was gone.

He jumped up, strong again, ready for anything again. He crouched, his hands poised for deadly attack. D'Andrea would believe him or be smashed as everyone who opposed him had been smashed. 'You believe me, don't you? Don't you?'

He leaped forward, screaming his *keeyi* ... and was launched into oblivion.

Bestsellers available in Panther Books

Emmanuelle Arsan

Emmanuelle	£1.95	☐
Emmanuelle 2	£1.95	☐
Laure	£1.95	☐
Nea	£1.95	☐
Vanna	£1.95	☐
The Secrets of Emmanuelle (non-fiction)	95p	☐

Jonathan Black

Ride the Golden Tiger	£1.95	☐
Oil	£1.95	☐
The World Rapers	£1.95	☐
The House on the Hill	£1.95	☐
Megacorp	£2.50	☐
The Plunderers	£2.50	☐

Herbert Kastle

Cross-Country	£2.50	☐
Little Love	£1.95	☐
Millionaires	£1.95	☐
Miami Golden Boy	£1.95	☐
The Movie Maker	£2.50	☐
The Gang	£1.95	☐
Hit Squad	£1.95	☐
Dirty Movies	£1.95	☐
Hot Prowl	£1.50	☐
Sunset People	£1.95	☐
David's War	£1.95	☐

To order direct from the publisher just tick the titles you want
and fill in the order form.

All these books are available at your local bookshop or newsagent, or can be ordered direct from the publisher.